ONE ON ONE
The Second Buddy Steel Mystery

"Another great read. Buddy Steel is my kind of Sheriff."

—Tom Selleck

"Buddy is a likable character who uses self-deprecating humor, sometimes acting like an overgrown schoolboy. He is easygoing and can handle people poking fun at him. Being smart, caring, and understanding of people's emotional pain, Buddy has a moral sense of right versus wrong. Readers will enjoy this fast-paced mystery. With well-developed characters and a plot that takes issues straight from the headlines, this is a good read."

—*Crimespree Magazine*

MISSING PERSONS
The First Buddy Steel Mystery

"*Missing Persons* is a cracking series debut and Buddy Steel is a protagonist bound to have a long shelf life."

—Reed Farrel Coleman, *New York Times* bestselling author
of *What You Break*

"Fans of Parker's work will appreciate Buddy, another irreverent, complex lawman."

—*Library Journal*

"Michael Brandman's follow-up to the three Jesse Stone novels he adeptly penned for the late Robert B. Parker gives us the cool and iconic Buddy Steel. A former point guard turned cop, Steel damn sure owns the ground he walks on. All capable 6'3" and one-hundred-seventy pounds of him, Buddy's that guy that you want to ride with when s..t hits the fan. With plenty of thrilling moments and turns you don't see coming, what a great ride Brandman takes us on in *Missing Persons*. Trust me, you won't be disappointed. Buckle up."

—Robert Knott, *New York Times* bestselling author
of The Hitch and Cole Series

WILD
CARD

WILD CARD

A Buddy Steel Mystery

MICHAEL BRANDMAN

Poisoned Pen
PRESS

Published by Poisoned Pen Press, an imprint of Sourcebooks
P.O. Box 4410, Naperville, Illinois 60563-4410
(630) 961-3900
sourcebooks.com

Library of Congress Cataloging 2018959455

Printed and bound in the United States of America.
SB 10 9 8 7 6 5 4 3 2 1

For Joanna...

*...who brightens the darkness
and shows me the way...*

...and for Sadie

"Politicians and diapers must be changed often,
and for the same reason."

—*Mark Twain*

ONE

They found the woman's body slumped over the steering wheel of a late-model Mercedes. A bullet fired through the driver's side window splattered glass, bone, and matter throughout the interior.

Sheriff's deputies Al Striar and Buzz Farmer spotted the sedan parked at an odd angle on Glasgow Street in the heart of downtown Freedom. The sedan's front end was poking into the road, forcing traffic to pull around it in order to get by. They phoned it in and sealed the area.

Departmental Dispatcher Wilma Hansen found me in my cruiser, parked on Overlook Drive in the Freedom foothills, catching up on the morning reports, a takeout coffee in my cup holder, a breathtaking view of the Pacific before me.

"We have a bad one," Wilma informed me.

"A bad one what?"

"Youngish woman. Dead in her vehicle. Shot in the head."

"Where?"

"Glasgow Street."

"Have they secured the site?"

"What does a bear do in the woods?"

"I'll take that as a yes."

"You never fail to impress, Buddy."

"Ditto." I ended the call.

• ● ● ● •

Glasgow Street was located in the heart of the financial district, home to a number of prominent bank branches and investment institutions. Traffic had been diverted away from the site which was causing backups and delays. I inched my way there with my finger on the siren trigger, sporadically blasting it as a signal to complacent drivers to move out of my way.

Several police cars and an ambulance were already at the scene when I arrived. Al Striar and Buzz Farmer met me.

"Looks like an assassination," Farmer commented.

He was new to the department, recruited from a list of experienced candidates, most, like him, from out of state. He was a presentable-looking thirtysomething, neatly groomed, nearly handsome, rusty-haired with a body sculpted by considerable training and exercise. He had done a single tour in Afghanistan and then returned home to Chicago, where his wife and young son awaited him. As did a position with the Chicago PD Homicide Division.

When he learned of the opening here in Freedom, and wishing to move his family west, away from the crime-riddled streets of the inner city, he leapt at it.

With Farmer at my side, I examined the scene in search of any clue that might lead us to an understanding of what exactly happened. Other than the strange angle in which the car was parked, nothing caught my attention. There was no indication of a struggle. It puzzled me.

"I don't know, Buzz. Could be anything. Woman alone in a fancy car. Commercial neighborhood. No visible clues. Let's ID her. And the car. See what we learn."

"It's pretty messy in there, Buddy. Should we let the forensics team in?"

"Might as well."

"This could require some time."

"What doesn't?"

TWO

I was staring out my office window with my feet up, not really seeing anything, mulling over the unlikely occurrence of a random killing here in Freedom, a mostly upscale residential community, second home to a number of entertainment industry and Silicon Valley luminaries.

I'm Buddy Steel, by the way. Actually, Burton Steel, Junior. But I prefer Buddy. I'm the nominal Sheriff of San Remo County, serving under my father, guarding the fort, so to speak, while he battles a serious illness.

San Remo County wasn't the future I had envisioned for myself. I was an LAPD Homicide detective when my father took ill. Now I'm here. Conflicted, I might add. Torn between a sense of familial duty and a desire to be anywhere else in the world except here.

Sometimes…late at night…when sleep is at its most elusive… I consider how the trajectory of my life changed so suddenly and so drastically. I had been summoned to my father's house for a family powwow, the one in which he formally announced his illness. ALS. Lou Gehrig's disease. "A fucking death sentence," he stoically unloaded.

Although he publicly scoffed at his alleged fate, when he got me alone he expressed his fear that everything he achieved over the course of his heady career would erode as he *slid into oblivion*. His words, not mine.

In the heat of the moment he implored me to stand with him and shield him from the scrutiny that would surely befall him as he publicly declined.

It was all about him, of course. It never occurred to him that were I to accede to his wishes it would put an end to the career trajectory I had painstakingly structured for myself and so greatly cherished.

In the end, however, it was the guilt that did it.

Having always been thought of as the wayward son, I finally caved when he insisted this was the last chance we would have to come to grips with our myriad differences.

In other words, he shamed me.

And I bought it.

Now I have days similar to those of my childhood. Not good ones, mind you. Days when I feel as I did growing up under the thumb of paternal tyranny. His way or the highway. Worse even after my mother died. The very reason I left here in the first place.

Captain Marsha Russo strolled into my office, plopped herself down across from me and waved an official-looking document. "Here's one I'm sure you'll enjoy."

"What is it?"

"Official document. Looks like very important stuff."

"What kind of stuff?"

"Important stuff."

"Did it ever cross your mind when you popped in here that I might be busy?"

She shook her head. "No. It never did."

"What exactly is this document?"

"Notice from the California Coastal Commission."

"Regarding?"

"The violation of state oceanfront access rules happening right here in San Remo County."

"What does it say?"

"Mentions someone called Boris Petrov. Some big deal Russian oligarch. Allegedly a Putin pal. Has film interests in Hollywood. What's this about, Buddy?"

"Do you remember the Stein estate?"

Marsha thought for a few moments. "I do remember it. Huge parcel of beachfront property. Sold for a record amount. Made the news big-time."

"It was this Petrov character who bought it. Turns out he doesn't see eye to eye with the Coastal Commission regarding the public's right to access the beach."

"So?"

"So, there's a problem. A couple of years back, when the Commission realized he was denying beach access to the common people, they sued. Suit was settled for a pittance and everyone thought the problem was resolved."

"Was it?"

"Nope. Turns out he battened the hatches. Sealed off the access points. Fences. Gates. Barbed wire. Security personnel. You know, the *screw you* approach."

"And that's of interest to us because?"

"We've been pegged by the Coastal Commission to help them enforce the law. Petrov's property is located in our county and the Commissioners want the previously designated access points re-opened and made available to the public."

"What do you mean *pegged*?"

"We've been enlisted by the Commission to assist them in their efforts to right the Petrov wrongs."

"And that's legal?"

"You mean for us to work with the Coastal Commission?"

"Yeah. That."

"There's ample precedent."

"And Petrov? How's he reacting to all this?"

"He's not."

"What do you mean *not*?"

"In gangland terms, he's gone to ground. Refusing to engage in any dialogue with the Commissioners."

"Despite the law?"

"He doesn't seem to recognize the law."

"That's a problem."

"Right."

"And now it's our problem."

"Got that right, too."

THREE

After studying the complaint, I decided to have a look at the place for myself. I rounded up Sheriff's Deputy Johnny Kennerly and together we headed for the southernmost tip of the county and the Petrov property.

Johnny is the Sheriff's longtime protégé, a good-looking rugged man of color, close to my age, wise beyond his years and deeply devoted to my father.

Some have suggested we're rivals for my father's attention and his blessings, but truth be known, his benevolence is of no interest to me. I'm more than delighted that Johnny is so close to him. It saves me a good deal of grief. And family stress.

"As I remember it," I said to Johnny as we drove south on Highway One, "this is a large parcel of land. Arguably one of the finest beachfront properties in the county. Pristine except for the garish mansion the Steins put up all those years ago."

"Did the Steins allow public access?"

"Apparently, they did. It was never a problem for them. It's a fair distance from the touristy Santa Barbara beaches. It's isolated. Not much of an attraction."

"Except for the beach."

"Except for that."

"So why would it be a problem for Mr. Petrov?"

"He doesn't seem to want to share his land with anyone else. Regardless of the law."

"Why, do you suppose?"

"That's what I'd like to find out."

• • ● • •

The Petrov estate was extravagant beyond even my expectations. The lengthy shoreline was an erratic blend of small inlets, hidden coves, massive dunes, stretches of immaculate beachfront, and a mansion the size of a small country.

It was reached by a palm tree-lined beachfront road that abutted the coast, separated from it by eight-foot-tall wrought iron fencing with barbed wire strung along the top.

A guardhouse stood in front of the main gate. Two gates, actually, electronically operated, opening inward. A fenced walkway was adjacent to the guardhouse.

As we arrived, a giant of a man stepped from the guardhouse and planted himself in front of it, silently watching us.

We exited our cruiser and approached the malevolent-looking guard who wore a khaki uniform with a kit belt that included a holstered Glock semi-automatic pistol, a nightstick, a walkie-talkie, a cell phone, and a pair of handcuffs. The name tag on his shirt read *VOLYA KOSKOFF*. He regarded us as if we were an enemy.

I knew Koskoff would be uncooperative. His dress and his demeanor were dead giveaways. I decided to test his mettle just the same. Tweak him a bit. Gauge his reaction.

"We're here to see Mr. Petrov."

Volya Koskoff shook his head.

I showed him my badge. "Sheriff's business."

Koskoff stared at me blank-eyed.

"Do you speak?"

No response.

"Read my lips. We want to see Mr. Petrov."

The guard shook his head. "No here," he barked in a thick Russian accent.

"When will he be here?"

He shrugged.

I shook my head. "This is a very unsatisfying conversation."

Koskoff stared at me a while longer, then turned and went back inside the guardhouse.

I stepped over to it and rang the bell. Inside, Koskoff was on the phone. After several moments, he stepped back outside, flashed me a sideways glance, climbed into a parked electric golf cart, and drove away.

Johnny and I exchanged looks. "That went well," he observed. "If this is any indication, we're in for some rough sailing with these shitbirds."

"Tell me about it."

FOUR

"The victim was a woman in her thirties. Julia Murphy. Wife of Harold Murphy, a Silicon Valley tech engineer. Parents of two teenage sons."

We were in my office, Al Striar, Buzz Farmer, and I. Farmer was reading from notes he had made earlier. "Husband's distraught. Can't imagine why this happened. Says she has no known enemies. Claims she had an appointment at the bank."

"And?"

"His story checks out. She did her banking and, as best Forensics can figure, she was pulling out of the parking space when she was shot. Likely someone approached the car, shot her through the window, and vanished."

"Security cameras?"

"Nonexistent where she was shot."

"What was she doing at the bank?"

"Signing a mortgage refinance agreement."

"They had financial difficulties?"

"On the contrary. They were reducing the size of their mortgage. Seems they were doing quite well."

"What do you think?"

"I don't know what to think, Buddy," Farmer said with the authority of someone who had been down this road many times before.

"We'll need to investigate further, but all things considered, this one's a bitch."

"What about the husband?"

"Not a likely candidate. He's a tech nerd and, from what we're learning, a successful one. And a devoted husband and father."

"You'll keep digging."

"For sure."

"I'm sensing a *but* in there somewhere."

Farmer glanced briefly at Striar, then back at me. "I don't like it."

"Because?"

"It defies logic."

"And?"

"As we learned in Afghanistan, things that defy logic tend to be worse than they first appear."

"Which means?"

"Just that, Buddy. Just that."

FIVE

The California Coastal Commission was established by voter initiative in 1972. Among its myriad responsibilities is the supervision of public access to the state shoreline, which can be problematic due to the entitlement that many of the smug and self-serving coastline homeowners exhibit when it comes to strangers sniffing around on what they perceive to be their own private beaches.

Denied access to beaches is one of the Commission's most frequent problems. The goal of the Coastal Access Program is to maximize public ingress to and along the coast and to insure public recreational opportunities in the coastal zone.

I'm a Southern Californian by birth and, aside from four years in New York City studying Criminology at John Jay College, I've been here all my life.

I grew up in the city of Freedom and was more than familiar with the fabled California Coastal Commission and its track record of financial misconduct. Coastal Commissioners were known to be sympathetic to the starry, monied, self-centered celebrities who sought to bend regulations that applied to their properties.

A noted movie magnate once introduced a Coastal Commissioner as someone who was "*living in my pocket.*"

We were sitting in Marsha Russo's office cubicle, in front of her computer, looking at photos of the Petrov estate that had been taken when the Steins owned the property. There were four access points to the beach, two on the southernmost part and one on the northernmost tip, as well as the main entrance facing the mansion.

In the photos, all access points are clearly identifiable, each with a large open gate, two with wooden staircases descending from street level to the beach below, thereby easing the ingress. The beach road provided ample parking. No barriers nor obstacles denied access.

Photos taken more recently, however, reveal no visible access. High wrought iron fencing runs the length of the property. The only access point is the main entrance, which is supervised by armed guards.

I couldn't help but wonder what Petrov was up to. It's one thing to deny beach access to strangers, but quite another to create fortress-like conditions to insure they stayed away.

"What next?" Johnny Kennerly asked.

"Search warrant."

"They won't accept service."

"We'll see about that."

"Mark my words, Buddy. You'll be left holding a warrant you can't serve."

"Duly marked."

I stopped in to visit my father, the estimable Sheriff, now hampered by the progressive neurodegenerative illness that affects nerve cells in the brain and the spinal cord.

Although there's no known cure for ALS, the Sheriff had recently become involved in the medical trial of a so-called miracle drug that claimed to slow its progress. He only recently began this therapy and was cautiously optimistic about its results.

He was seated on the screened in back porch of the family manse, relishing the warmth of the late spring day, the air ripe with the pungent smell of jasmine. He was sipping lemonade from his favorite glass, the one he had been presented with at Disneyland, the one with Mickey inanely grinning at him. "I'm hearing you have your hands full."

"You could say that, yes."

"What do you think?"

"I think I'd rather not have my hands full."

"Is this going to be wise guy day around here?"

The old man had no patience for those he judged to be wise guys. And although I was more than familiar with his means of retribution, at this point in our ongoing saga I couldn't resist even the slightest chance to bust his chops. If only to ascertain his reaction.

I shrugged.

"You think we could serious up, Buddy?"

I nodded.

"Tell me about this killing."

"I'm afraid we don't know a whole lot other than it happened."

"Suspects?"

"None."

"Ideas?"

"None."

"So what's next?"

"I've appointed the new guy, Buzz Farmer, to head the investigation. He's pretty much at the starting line."

"The press is going to want answers."

"Me, too."

He glared at me. "And the Coastal Commission thing?"

"Also at the starting line."

"You know he's a litigious bastard. Mean-spirited, too," the old man offered.

"Petrov?"

"Yes. Him. What's your plan?"

"Search warrant, for openers."

"Dubious. He's got any number of high-priced lawyers who will be all over it trying to quash it."

"I'm shaking like a leaf."

"I'm serious, Buddy. You haven't encountered anyone like him before."

"Ditto."

The old man took a sip of lemonade and pointed to the pitcher on the side table. "Lemonade?"

"I'm good. Thanks."

"Have you asked yourself why the Commission decided to act now?"

"Why do you think?"

He shifted in his seat, struggling to make himself comfortable. "Because of you."

"What does that mean?"

"You have no skin in this game, Buddy. You're a wild card. You're here to support me during my illness. You weren't elected to the job, like I was. You have no political agenda and you're answerable only to yourself.

"The Commissioners know you're tough-minded and non-conventional. They believe you can stand up to this Russian bastard and to anything he might throw at you."

"And they can't?"

"They don't want to be in the front lines of any unpleasantness involving Mr. Petrov."

"Because?"

"He's got friends in high places."

"So?"

"So, use the authority they provide you and do what it takes. Once you restore the public access, you'll be a hero."

"If I survive, you mean."

"You'll survive. Just keep in mind the old adage."

"Which is?"

"Shoot first and ask questions later."

SIX

"This could stir up the hornet's nest," Judge Ezekiel Azenberg said as he signed the warrant.

"You think?"

Weathered, craggy-faced, and generally cranky, Judge Azenberg leaned back in his worn, overstuffed leather chair. We were in his chambers, a dreary place adjacent to his courtroom. "A word to the wise?"

"That sounds ominous."

"This Petrov bird, he struts around like he's Russian aristocracy. Has a different attorney for every possibility and isn't the least bit reluctant to gum up the works with lawsuits. Sometimes they get thrown out. Sometimes he withdraws them. He's never ready for trial and always seeks delays. He's unpredictable and vexing. And mean. He won't take kindly to this."

"Sounds like a challenge."

"No more so than the Coastal Commission."

"Meaning?"

"I'm sure you're aware of their checkered reputation. Conflicts of interest. Collusion with big-time developers. Payoffs under the table. More than a few Commissioners have been indicted. Now they've handed you a hot potato, Buddy. One they couldn't suppress any longer. I'm thinking there's some subtext at play here.

Your presence in this game puts unexpected distance between them and Boris Petrov."

"Which suggests?"

"Off the record?"

I nodded.

"They could be setting you up. Washing their hands of this matter by handing it off to you. Keep your eyes open, Buddy. Do what you have to do, but don't trust any of these snakes."

"That's quite a word to the wise."

"It is what it is."

●●●●●

I arrived before dawn, parked in front of the guardhouse and rang the bell. Then I hid in the shadows by the side of the fenced walkway, invisible in the early morning darkness.

My intention was less about serving Judge Azenberg's warrant than it was about sending a message to Boris Petrov. I wanted him to know that two could play his game. And despite his plethora of security personnel, he would never trump American jurisprudence. No pun intended.

After a while Volya Koskoff arrived in a golf cart. He got off and stood silently for several moments, gazing around. Then he drew the pistol from his kit belt and holding it by his side, slowly approached the gate.

He glanced into the shadows but didn't spot me. He did notice the Wrangler however.

He opened the gate and stepped through it. He continued to scan the area, but still didn't see me. He moved stealthily toward the Wrangler.

I suddenly bolted from the darkness and dashed in his direction, which startled him. I slapped the pistol from his hand and kicked it away.

Then I stuffed the warrant into his shirt pocket. I pulled out my cell phone and snapped a photo of him.

When he focused on me, recognition slowly dawned. "You've been served," I said.

I stepped swiftly to the Wrangler and jumped in. I fired up the engine and lowered the passenger-side window. I grinned at him. "Have a nice day."

I sped off.

SEVEN

Buzz Farmer picked me up at seven. We were each decked out in our finest, headed for Blau's Mortuary where the Murphy family was receiving friends and relatives.

I hadn't before shared any official events with him, but Buzz cleaned up well and looked impressive in a tailored black suit. He seemed a tad nervous but I attributed that to his new surroundings and lack of familiarity with local protocols.

After evading the handful of reporters who shouted questions at us from behind a hastily erected barrier, we were met at the door and quickly ushered inside by Julian Blau, the son of the mortuary's proprietor, a longtime friend from our school days. "A terrible tragedy," Julian volunteered.

I nodded.

"It's a tough room in there, Buddy. I hope you're not planning to stir the pot."

"Why would you say a thing like that?"

"Because I know you."

"We're here to pay our respects."

Julian stared at me. "You're not going to start grilling the assembled?"

"You've seen too many cop shows, Julian."

He led us into the viewing room, decorated with somber-looking drapes of muted colors. A closed walnut casket stood on a catafalque at the far end of the room, adjacent to a sitting area for the family, comprised of half a dozen armchairs, all occupied.

A thin man with thick glasses and an ill-fitting brown suit sat in the center. A pair of teen-aged boys, also in brown suits, sat on either side of him. Buzz identified them as the deceased's immediate family.

We stood at the back of the room, watching the goings on. Numbers of mourners, many of them in tears, were doing their best to comfort the grieving family and each other.

After a while, we approached the brown-suited man who stood and looked at me questioningly when I offered my hand.

"Hal Murphy," he murmured.

"Buddy Steel. I wanted to offer our condolences and assure you the Sheriff's Department is putting all of its resources into the investigation of this heinous crime."

"You came here to tell us that?"

"We came to pay our respects."

"That's very kind of you, Sheriff."

I handed him one of my cards. "All of my numbers are on it. Please feel free to call at any time. We'll schedule a more formal interview later."

We shook hands once again and I also shook hands with each of the boys, both of whom looked at me through red-rimmed eyes.

We were watched by several mourners, many of whom nodded to us as we made our way out of the mortuary.

When we reached the lobby, we encountered Her Honor, Freedom Mayor Regina Goodnow, my stepmother, making a grand entrance, accompanied by two of her legislative assistants and several City Councilpersons.

There was nothing understated about Regina. She was meticulously coiffed, elegantly dressed in various degrees of black, and wearing only those few pieces of her vast jewelry collection she deemed appropriate for the occasion.

As usual, she regarded me warily. We have a tenuous relation-ship, Regina and I. In many ways we're like sparring partners, nimbly dancing around each other in search of vulnerabilities.

"Buddy," she erupted when she spotted me. "What a surprise."

"Likewise."

She kissed me on both cheeks. "You're here because?"

"To pay our respects to the bereaved family."

She looked at me quizzically.

"You find that strange?" I asked.

"Not in the least. It's what your father would have done."

Ever the political animal, her eyes darted here and there in search of anyone present whom she might want to acknowledge or impress.

Her attentions returned to me. She waved her hand. "I'll be in touch. We need to schedule a dinner."

After kissing me on both cheeks again, and shaking Buzz's hand, she motioned to her acolytes and together they moved off.

As I watched her go, I was once again struck by her imperious-ness. And by how different she was from my mother. I wondered how I would have turned out had I weighed my life choices in concert with my mother's counsel, as opposed to Regina's.

"Is it what your father would have done?" Buzz asked.

"It is, if she says it is."

EIGHT

I agreed to meet Coastal Commissioner James Morrison in Malibu. He had driven up from his base in Long Beach. We were sipping coffee and nibbling donuts at the Malibu Pier Cafe, overlooking the Pacific and within sight of the legendary Colony, home to a glut of Hollywood celebrities and eccentrics.

The drive on Highway 101 from Freedom filled me with renewed sadness as I witnessed the devastation wrought by the Woolsey fires late last year. Vast sections of the once verdant mountainside lay charred, the burnt skeletons of homes and businesses dotting the roadside as symbols of the fragile nature of life and property.

The sky was pockmarked with clouds and the sun revealed itself only sporadically. A chill wind carried with it the faint smell of rancid smoke. Both of us had on pea coats. Morrison wore a Dodgers cap, I a Russian sailor's.

"You certainly caught his attention," the Commissioner said between bites of a glazed cruller. "His lawyers are headed to court."

"For what purpose?"

"To quash the warrant."

"Doesn't the Commission hold the upper hand here?"

"You'd think. The law couldn't be clearer. But the estimable

Craig Leonard of the firm Leonard, Howard and Arthur, Attorneys at Law, is screaming desecration of a wildlife preserve. He claims that unwarranted access to the property will destroy the ecological balance his client has been striving so hard to protect. A crock of shit, if you ask me."

Morrison was a slight man with a gentle demeanor. He had been appointed to the Commission after the fall of two of his predecessors for alleged conflicts of interest.

They had chummed up with a well-known rock musician who sought to build five oversized mansions on a heretofore undeveloped hilltop overlooking the ocean. On property that wasn't permitted for such development. The whole deal stunk to the high heavens. Rumors of payoffs were rampant. When the plans reached the Governor's desk, he denied the permits and fired the two Commissioners.

He then appointed Morrison as a replacement, allegedly to right the corrupted ship. But there was already dissension in the ranks of the elected Commissioners, a number of whom sounded keen to defy the Governor and arrange a special election to fill the seats.

A practicalist, Morrison shrugged off any possible ill feelings regarding the uncertainty of his position. He knew full well that over the years, numbers of Coastal Commissioners had been rumored to have lived largely in the pockets of affluent landowners and voracious developers. He was anathema to that ethic, and as a result, more than likely a short-timer. But he took his position seriously and soldiered on nonetheless.

I pressed him. "So what happens next?"

"Delays followed by even more delays."

"And Petrov can get away with it?"

"It's what he's paying for."

Morrison finished his cruller and wiped his hands. He eyed me and lowered his voice. "I never said what I'm about to tell you."

I nodded.

"There's a way to force the issue."

"And that would be?"

"We re-create the old access points."

"And we would do that how?"

"We would tear down the fences that block the access points. Or, rather, you would."

"And the aforementioned Leonard, Howard and Blah Blah?"

"They'd take us to court."

"Us being?"

"The Commission."

"So the Coastal Commission would be hauled into court for upholding its laws?"

Morrison nodded.

I shook my head, acknowledging that the exploits of the Coastal Commission were often frustratingly obtuse. "Seems a bit loony, don't you think?"

"I do."

"And they want to go forward with this action, regardless of the consequences?"

"Half of the Commissioners want to take this Russki bastard down a peg."

"And the other half?"

"Don't ask."

"What's that supposed to mean?"

"The Commission is known for its checkered history."

"Corruption?"

He looked away and waved his hand. "I never said that. But for the moment, it's a good time to take action. In large part because there's no way of knowing how much longer I'll be able to hold my seat. And I'm currently *it* insofar as the majority vote is concerned."

I sat back and mulled for a while. I watched a gull land on the deck near us, its focus on a section of cruller that Morrison had inadvertently dropped. Sensing his moment, the gull dashed for the cruller, grabbed it, and without even a glance at us, swooped away.

"Okay," I said.

"Okay what?"

"I'll do it."

"So maybe some good will come from our conversation."

"What conversation?"

NINE

I was strolling along South Freedom Beach in the company of my lifelong friend, the Assistant District Attorney Skip Wilder. Both of us were barefoot, wearing baggy canvas shorts and, although unplanned, Freedom High sweatshirts.

For privacy reasons Wilder had suggested we meet on this remote stretch of undeveloped shoreline, a favorite haunt of our youth. The sun felt warm on our pale winter faces, a harbinger, perhaps, of summer to come.

I picked up a small rock and hurled it into the sea, then turned to face him. "I need an opinion."

"Find a new line of work."

"Funny."

"So, what's up?"

"The Sheriff's Department was asked to work with the Coastal Commission to help rectify a problem."

"The Commission needs help in enforcing the law?"

"Here in San Remo County? Yes."

"So?"

"It's more problematic than they had let on."

"Problematic how?"

"There's an access violation which the homeowner is refusing to acknowledge."

"So, warrant the sucker and do what you need to do."

"Easier said than done."

"Because?"

"Boris Petrov is because."

"Boris Petrov?"

"Him."

"Him and his team of legal pit bulls, you mean."

"Here's the conundrum, Skip. Petrov's attorneys are bringing suit to prevent the Commission from upholding the law."

"What a nifty concept."

"So, what do I do?"

"What does your gut tell you to do?"

"Tear down the fences and open the access points."

"So, do it."

"And the lawsuit?"

"Not your problem."

"What do you mean?"

"If you're asking my legal opinion, I'm opining that you'd be defending and upholding the existing laws, and if Mr. Petrov is unhappy about it, tough noogies. Let him take on the Coastal Commission, the State of California, hell, even the Easter Bunny, for all I care. You're well within your rights."

"And you'll stand behind this opinion?"

"I never said that."

"Come on, Skip. Will you stand behind it?"

"Look, Buddy. You asked me here to render an opinion. I'm not here in any official capacity. Before I could officially render an opinion, I'd have to consult the District Attorney and possibly even the State's Attorney."

"So this was a big waste of time."

"Not in the least. You can trust my opinion. You just can't reference it as justification for any action you might take."

"Lawyers," I muttered. "No wonder you're reviled."

"Also revered."

"Maybe in some quarters."

"You can fool some of the people some of the time," Wilder snickered.

TEN

It was a sleepless one. Try as I might, I couldn't get the thought of the Murphy family out of my head. I was of the same mind as Buzz Farmer. The husband didn't do it. But that being the case, who did?

Buzz instinctively felt wary about it. Almost as if he were waiting for another shoe to drop. But from the looks of it, that shoe might not drop straight away, if ever, leaving us with an open unsolved that wouldn't sit well with the County.

I was also priming myself for what would surely be a furball regarding Boris Petrov. Although it wasn't unusual for the Coastal Commission to enlist local law enforcement to assist with access issues, the threat posed by Team Petrov was.

I could envision time and resources being swallowed by the exigencies of keeping up with the Petrov contingent. The pitfalls of small-town policing…time and money.

My focus as an LAPD homicide detective was sharply defined, whereas that of a County Sheriff is all over the map. My father averred that every small-town day brought with it a new and unusual challenge. Far more intriguing than the narrow focus of big-city policing. As with most things, however, he and I disagreed.

He thinks a career with a big town police force is a dead end.

The equivalent of a prison sentence. Serve your time, collect your pension, go home to die. He says I'm far better off in San Remo County.

He believes that one or two big cases in a small force will raise my profile, thereby enhancing my career and elevating my chances for higher office. He's even mouthed the word Governor. But that's his vision, not mine.

In fact, as I get deeper into serving as de facto Sheriff, the whole business becomes less and less appealing.

It's not that I have other choices. It's that I'm second-guessing the efficacy of my original ones and I'm starting to come up cold.

I have begun to challenge myself as to whether I want to remain on the law enforcement ride, or bail and find something completely different. As of now, I have no answers.

But it's days like this…days when I wake up and realize that what I'm facing is the kind of mind-numbing tedium that inhibits ingenuity and saps energy.

I continued to rail against myself until the first rays of light seeped through the blinds and I rolled out of bed.

ELEVEN

We moved in at dawn on the southernmost tip of the Petrov property on the beach road, the site of one of the original access points.

A BearCat battering ram operated by Sheriff's Deputy P.J. Lincoln succeeded in bringing down a section of the wrought iron fence that blocked access to the beach.

After pushing the downed fence and its barbed-wire accoutrements away from the site, the battering ram also brought down a fifty-foot section of thick laurel hedging that had been planted inside the fencing to deny any visual access to the beach.

With the fence and the hedging now gone, an access point had been re-created. A team of officers swept the area, removing whatever debris remained. A signpost was planted at the site heralding it as a Beach Access point. A *Parking Allowed* signpost with access times delineated now stood at the roadside.

Satisfied, I was in the process of sending the BearCat and the team of deputies ahead to the second target when I spotted a pair of SUVs steaming down the beach road in our direction.

After instructing the team to spread out in front of the access site, I stepped up to the road just as the lead vehicle screeched to a stop. A cluster of uniformed Petrov security personnel leapt from the SUVs and moved to confront us. Their leader was Volya Koskoff.

He stormed up and stood chest-to-chest with me, close enough for me to get a face full of his foul-smelling breath. "Private property," he squawked in his thick accent.

I stared at him cold-eyed. When I didn't speak, he became agitated.

"This is private beach. You leave. Now."

I wondered how far Koskoff was prepared to go in defense of Boris Petrov. He had to realize he was rapidly approaching a tipping point and for him, were he here illegally, that tipping point could well portend his future, not only with Petrov, but, more importantly, here in America. I decided to torment him further.

I produced a photocopy of the original search warrant and waved it under his nose. "Perhaps this will refresh your memory."

I then produced a copy of the Coastal Commission's order and stuffed it into his shirt pocket. "Contrary to your opinion, Mr. Koskoff, the beach is no longer private property."

Flabbergasted, Koskoff stood silently, uncertain of what to do next. He turned to one of his associates, a tough-looking thug with an equally menacing appearance. Whether or not the thug interpreted Koskoff's glance as a signal to action, he nonetheless approached me and, without warning, shoved me, causing me to stumble and fall backward.

It was then that Johnny Kennerly produced his X26 Taser and fired at him. I watched the electric current dance all over the man's body, causing him both pain and neuromuscular incapacitation. He flopped to the ground, his body experiencing involuntarily muscular contractions.

When Koskoff made an inadvertent move in my direction, Johnny tasered him, too. In short order, both men were on the ground, which is where Deputy Al Striar cuffed them.

"When they calm down, read them their rights and arrest them. For assaulting an officer of the law. Once they've been jailed, check their IDs with Immigration and Customs Enforcement. My money says they're in the country illegally."

I gave the remaining security personnel the once-over. "Anyone else?"

One of them signaled for the others to get back into their vehicles. They hightailed it away.

I watched as Striar and Johnny loaded Koskoff and his associate into a Sheriff's van. After bolting them each to the floor, Striar climbed in and drove off with sirens blaring.

"What's next?" Johnny asked.

"We open the other access points."

"You think there'll be interference?"

"Not likely yet."

"When?"

"If any of those thugs speak English, I'd be guessing soon. But the threat won't come from them. Beware the lawyers."

"Injunctions?"

"Likely."

"What do we do?"

"For now I'm recommending we turn off our cell phones."

"Because?"

"That way they can't reach us. If they can't contact us by phone, they'll have to send people to serve us personally, who, by the way, will never make it out here before we finish the job."

"Sweet," Johnny said.

"Sweet, if no one shows up."

"And if they do?"

"As my father instructed, *Shoot first and ask questions later.*"

TWELVE

We had liberated the second access point in the southern part of the property and were just arriving at the main entrance when I spotted one of our Sheriff's cruisers screaming toward us, sirens blaring. When Captain Marsha Russo reached us, she got out of her cruiser and waved. "Something's wrong with your phones," she shouted.

I smiled. "They're off."

"Your phones are off?"

I nodded.

"All of them?"

I nodded again.

"What are you, nuts? We've been trying to reach you."

"Petrov and Company have filed an injunction," I said, almost simultaneously with Marsha's own pronouncement, "Because Petrov and Company have filed an injunction."

Again I smiled.

Marsha looked at me. "I'm sorry. What did you just say?"

"The injunction."

"How could you have known?"

"I'm a Sheriff. I know everything."

"Very funny, Buddy. Mr. Lytell is desperate to speak with you."

"Figures."

"What do you mean, figures?"

"He was unprepared."

"Unprepared for what?"

"This kind of action."

"You mean the tearing down fences kind of action?"

"Exactly."

"Why?"

"Why was he unprepared?"

Marsha nodded.

"Because the Commission wanted to re-open the access points before any lawyers got wise to it."

"Why?"

"It's a hot-button issue."

"The access points?"

I nodded.

"And you knew that when you came here."

"As I was directed to do by Commissioner Morrison."

Marsha looked at Johnny Kennerly then back at me. "Do you want to use my phone or will you turn yours back on?"

"Neither."

"What?"

"I have no business with the District Attorney. He needs to be in touch with the Coastal Commission. Any injunctive relief will have to be settled between him and them. I'm not going to be in the middle of it."

"So what do you want me to tell him?"

"Lytell?"

"Yes."

"Tell him you can't find me."

"You want me to tell him I can't find you."

"I just said that."

"Was there anything else?"

"Please inform the immigration authorities that I believe there's a ring of illegals working security at the Petrov mansion."

"You want ICE officers to investigate Petrov's employees?"

"I do."

"And you think he'll stand for it?"

"Mr. Petrov isn't here in any kind of official diplomatic role."

"Meaning?"

"He has no immunity."

"But he does have lawyers."

"They won't do him any good. If I'm right and his goons are here illegally, they're going to be thrown out of the country. And fast, too."

"And you really think that's going to happen?"

"I do."

"Because?"

"Illegal is illegal. And no fancy-pants lawyers can prove otherwise, regardless of whether or not their client is in cahoots with Vladimir Putin."

"Do you think you might be playing with fire here, Buddy?"

"Anything's possible."

THIRTEEN

"You certainly created a brouhaha," the Sheriff said.

He was experiencing the effects of the experimental ALS drug and feeling better. He was in his office and looked more energized than he had in weeks. "I've already heard from the DA and the Leonard, Howard and Arthur firm."

"Craig Leonard," I said.

"Yeah. Him. They're claiming trespassing, illegal search and seizure, and false arrest."

"Wow. The trifecta."

"This is serious business, Buddy. Try not to trivialize it."

"Did Immigration pick up the Russians?"

"If you're referring to Boris Petrov's security personnel, yes, they did."

"All of them?"

"Yes."

"Excellent. It should only be a matter of hours before they're all on a plane to Russia. That should make the job easier."

"What do you mean?"

"We have two more access points to clear and without those thugs to deter us, we can get it done straightaway."

"You can't go back there."

"Says who?"

"The Leonard, Howard and Arthur law firm."

"What does the Commission say?"

"Nothing yet."

"Then we still have a job to do."

"This is a major megillah, Buddy. I propose you bow out of it for the time being."

I stood and, in a rare moment of tenderness, walked over to the old man and kissed him on his forehead. He looked dazed, then he smiled.

"You're the one who said I'm a wild card. And as such, I've got my claws into this one big-time. At least until the Commission tells me otherwise."

"What about the District Attorney?"

"Not his table. At least not according to Commissioner Morrison. I say we carry on with our assignment and abide the events."

"The events?"

"Yes. And they'll more than likely prove to be highly entertaining."

"Ever the cynic," my father said.

"Ever."

• ● ● ● •

I jumped into my cruiser, heading for Bernie's Deli. It was my turn to pick up lunch. Wilma had already phoned in the order.

Bernie's was a local hot spot in a nearby strip mall. Parking was scarce so I pulled into a No Parking zone and made tracks for the deli.

The attack caught me off guard. A sharp metal object which I later learned was a tire iron, rang down heavily across my shoulders and neck, knocking me off my feet.

I looked up in time to see a squat fireplug of a man, dressed all in black, raise the tire iron and slam me with it again, this time in the lower back.

Despite the shock and the pain, I was able to wrest my Colt

commander from its holster before the man in black could strike me again.

As he raised the tire iron, I shot him, the .230-grain round tearing into his left hip with a vengeance, shattering it and slamming him backward into the wall behind him. He landed heavily, screaming in pain.

Responding to the sudden noise, a second man, also in black with a tire iron in his hand, made tracks for me.

Still in pain, I trained my pistol at him and hollered. "Stop or I'll shoot you. Put down the weapon."

The man glanced at his fallen comrade, then at me. He dropped the tire iron and raised his hands above his head.

I cautiously stood on wobbly legs and walked slowly toward him. When I reached him, without warning I smacked the gun hard into the side of his head. He collapsed in a heap.

I grabbed my cell phone and called the station. When Wilma answered, I hurriedly explained what had just gone down. I asked for backup and an ambulance.

Hoping that none of my bones had been broken, I weakly managed to flip the second assailant onto his stomach. I cuffed his hands behind him and secured his legs with the plastic tie I had on my kit belt.

I stepped over to the man I had shot. Blood from his wounded hip was seeping through his pants and pooling on the ground beneath him. He had lost consciousness. I speculated as to whether or not he would survive.

When I heard the second assailant moaning, I padded over to him, knelt beside him and searched his pockets, where I found a Smith & Wesson Bodyguard 380 semi-automatic pistol, which I removed and tossed aside. Then I lifted his wallet.

In the wallet I found a few hundred dollars in cash, a Master Card and an International driver's license, both issued in the name Vlad Smernik. His home was St. Petersburg, Russia. Still on his stomach, the man lifted his head and glared at me.

"Russian?" I inquired.

"Yes."

"What's this about?"

"We were sent to deliver a message. Rough you up a little. Scare you."

"Boris Petrov?"

He ignored my question and pointed to his downed associate. "You killed Misha?"

"Too soon to tell."

I heard sirens screaming in the distance. "Petrov?"

He nodded.

"Figures. Why is it you don't sound Russian?"

He struggled to get a better glimpse of me. "I was taught English by an American. When I was little. My grandmother."

"Your grandmother was an American?"

"Met and married my grandfather after the war."

"In Russia?"

"That's where she was stationed."

"Military?"

He nodded.

"And?"

"She renounced."

"Because?"

"My grandfather was a Communist."

"Sounds like a movie title."

"Do you actually give a shit?"

"Not really."

He was youthful-looking, stocky and muscular, dark-haired and brown-eyed. "I'm guessing this won't be ending well for me."

"Good guess."

"Jail?"

"More likely extradition."

He hung his head. Then he looked up at me. "You're some kind of big cheese around here, right?"

"And if I was?"

"Would you go easy on me?"

"Why would I do that?"

"Because you never know when inside information might be of use."

"What inside information?"

"I'm part of the Petrov security team."

"So?"

"I might have information that would be of interest to you."

"Regarding Petrov?"

"His ventures are very widespread and not always on the up and up. Things with him aren't as they appear."

"Meaning?"

"Think about my offer, Mr. Cheese. I could well become your new best friend."

A pair of squad cars and an ambulance arrived on the scene with sirens blaring. Four officers poured out of the two cars, one of whom was Johnny Kennerly.

I explained what happened. He looked at the downed men, then back at me.

"You all right?"

"Shaken up a bit. My shoulder doesn't feel so great."

We watched as the paramedics placed the wounded man onto a stretcher and loaded him into the ambulance. One of them gave me a thumbs-up, then got behind the wheel of the ambulance and raced off.

Johnny looked back at me. "Who are these guys?"

"Russians. Sent to deliver a message from Boris Petrov."

"What message?"

"Likely how my life would last longer if I tended to my own business."

"That was the message?"

"According to Vlad Smernik, it was."

"Who's Vlad Smernik?"

"That guy over there."

"So, now what?"

"The stakes have been raised."

"Raised how?"

"I think it may be time to wreak more discomfort onto our Mr. Petrov."

"If you can find him. Seems to keep himself well hidden."

"I'll find him. If I have to look under every rock on his estate, I'll find him."

FOURTEEN

"Not only have you been warned, you've also been served."

Skip Wilder had summoned me to his office, this time in his official capacity at Assistant District Attorney.

"Wow. Looks like I hit pay dirt."

"Don't wise around, Buddy. This is serious. I heard you were shaken up a bit."

I nodded.

"These guys aren't afraid to play rough. The service is from Leonard, Howard and Arthur on behalf of The Petrov Ecological Protection Society. They're claiming you trespassed on privately owned property and desecrated several acres dedicated to the preservation of indigenous wildlife and coastal integrity. They've also served the County of San Remo for aiding and abetting your crime."

"My crime? What about their crime?"

"They're denying Petrov had any hand in it."

"You mean they're saying these goons were acting on their own?"

"They admit their boys were out of line, but they maintain their actions weren't sanctioned by Petrov. That he had no knowledge of what they were up to."

"So in English what does this mean?"

"Lytell is in touch with the Coastal Commission and together they're preparing a countersuit. No permitting has ever been granted to any Petrov entity that would support their claims of coastal preservation protections. But they are in violation of Commission rules regarding public access to state-owned beaches."

"And the attack on me?"

"We'll see how they respond to the suit. In the meantime, one of the attackers has been jailed."

"And the other?"

"Hospitalized."

"So?"

"It will take time to go through the courts."

"Because?"

"Leonard and Company will exhaust every opportunity to stall the process."

"For how long?"

"Long."

"What does that mean for the access laws?"

"There's the rub. The Commission will claim that regardless of any lawsuits, the rules are the rules and Petrov is in violation of them."

"There's a *but* in there somewhere."

"The *but* is Petrov's perceived threat to his property and his person by strangers who wander onto his land."

"That's a load of crap."

"Tell that to the judge."

"Meaning?"

"The pockets of justice are stuffed with the spoils of corruption."

"And you think *I'm* cynical."

Wilder shifted in his seat and leaned closer to me. "A piece of personal advice."

"I'm not liking the sound of that."

"Nor should you. I'm suggesting you engage legal counsel."

"Why?"

"Odds are Petrov is seriously angry at you."

"Because?"

"You blew the whistle on nearly his entire security team."

"They're all illegals."

"Be that as it may, he's pissed."

"So he's pissed. Who cares?"

"You should. Lytell and Commissioner Morrison are of a mind to believe he's going to come after you."

"He's already done that."

"I mean legally. Your position will be in jeopardy. The press will be notified. The State's Attorney, too. He and his team will do everything they can to force you to step down."

"Because?"

"You weren't elected. Your father was. Petrov's lawyers will insist either he serve the term he was elected to serve or resign. They're likely to claim you have no official position and, as a result, no official job."

"That's also a load of crap."

"It is. And in the long haul, it won't hold up."

"But in the short haul?"

"It's anyone's guess."

"Hence an attorney."

"You catch on fast."

• ● ● ● •

I was at home, soaking my sore shoulder in a hot bath. So the game has grown nastier. Petrov wants my goose cooked. I wasn't elected. My father was. And either the old man shows up and does his business, or he gets pushed off the pot.

I got to thinking about Mr. Boris Petrov. The research confirms that his claim to credibility is due largely to his relationship with Vladimir Putin.

They allegedly joined forces in East Germany and then later in Moscow while working for the Fifth Chief Directorate, a unit of the KGB dedicated to crushing political dissidents. Together they made a vicious pair who stopped short of nothing in their efforts to quash dissent.

They quickly caught the attention of the then KGB boss Yuri Andropov, who sanctioned their use of torture, mutilation, and even murder as the most effective ways of achieving their goals. As their reputations grew, so did their power.

When Putin finally wrested control of the government away from Boris Yeltsin on the last day of the twentieth century, he quickly rewarded Petrov with money and status and, most importantly, access.

It was Putin who enabled Petrov to establish roots in America, where he gained a toehold in any number of businesses. But his primary value to Putin was as his eyes and ears.

Petrov was by nature more short-tempered and vindictive than his benefactor on whose coattails he so readily rode. While he embraced his newly found stature in the free world, his tenets were rooted in perfidy and retribution.

As I would come to learn, life in Petrov's sphere was more likely to continue unabated if it took place on his terms.

Despite Petrov's desire to upend me, in point of fact it doesn't much matter whether or not I hold onto the job. But it matters to my father and that's good enough for me. Although my heart isn't in it, I'm prepared to act like it is and fight for it.

Maybe not exactly for the job, but more so for the old man's legacy. He deserves to maintain the reins until it's no longer feasible. He served his constituency well, and as his surrogate, I'll continue to act in his behalf until fate intervenes.

Petrov's threats don't intimidate me. Neither legally nor physically. I'll engage counsel who will be stronger and tougher than his. I'll make certain his personal goon squad is depleted and deported.

I know he's vulnerable. I don't yet know how, but whatever he's hiding, I'm going to find it.

My pledge to my father stands. I have his back, and God help the son of a bitch who thinks I don't.

FIFTEEN

The second body was found on Scotland Road in downtown Freedom. Young woman shot in the head as she was pulling her BMW sedan away from the meter at which it had been parked. Front of the car was sticking out into the road.

Driver's side window shattered. Blood and matter bathed the interior. No visible clues.

Deputy Buzz Farmer met me at the scene. "Carbon copy," he said as we circled the BMW.

I admired Farmer's professionalism. His experiences in Chicago had honed his forensic skills. He conducted himself deferentially and with aplomb.

I remembered what it was that informed my decision to hire him. He had phoned my office on a Sunday morning. I was alone, poring over a handful of weekly reports. When I picked up the call, he identified himself and explained why he was calling. "I hope I'm not bothering you on a Sunday."

"Not at all. I like being here on Sunday. It's mostly quiet. Small-town quiet."

"It's the small-town quiet that's behind this call."

"Oh?"

"I'm just coming off shift. Another Chicago night. I don't even know the number of homicides. It remains a mystery to me as to why these gangs think killing someone is the best way to resolve issues. You know, when you take any one of them aside and try to have a reasonable conversation about it, by and large, they agree. No one wants to die."

"So what does that tell you?"

"Mostly it tells me that in an environment where life is cheap and easily taken, I'm in greater danger than what I deem to be reasonable."

"Meaning?"

"I have two little kids. I go to sleep fearing that one day I won't come home. And what will happen to them then?"

"And you're telling me this because?"

"I wanted you to know how much it would mean to me to be a member of your department. And not only me. It would mean the world to my family, as well."

"Thank you, Buzz. I will most assuredly take this into consideration."

"Thanks, Buddy. I'm very grateful."

After that it wasn't a difficult choice. He had an exemplary résumé. He was passionate about wanting the job. He was ecstatic when I announced my decision. He's been an excellent addition to the department.

"What do you make of it?" I asked him.

"I don't like the similarity."

"And?"

"I'll bet when we make contact with the next of kin the story will be the same as the first one."

"No motive."

"Except for one."

"Are you suggesting a serial motive?"

"I am."

"Damn."

We passed a forensics unit that was just beginning its examination of the scene. Stu Steinmark, the lead tech, looked at me and shook his head.

Farmer had entered the woman's purse into evidence and had

gathered the necessary information from her wallet. "You want to take a ride?"

"To her house?"

"Yes."

"Might as well."

"It won't be pleasant."

"It never is."

• ● ● ● •

Bonnie Weil lived in a two-family tract house in the Freedom foothills along with her sister, Meredith, a pair of miniature schnauzers and an ancient Siamese cat who had been with her since high school.

Meredith Weil answered the door and immediately surmised that our visit wasn't a good one. "What happened?"

She stepped back to allow us entry into her small living room. "She's dead, isn't she? I mean that's the only reason you guys ever just show up. Right?"

I nodded. "Our condolences, Ms. Weil."

She did her best to maintain her composure. She asked how it happened but began sobbing before we finished telling her. Devastated was an understatement.

"Is there anyone who might be available to be here with you?"

"You mean now?"

"Yes."

She thought for several moments. "Our brother and his wife live nearby."

Clearly this wasn't her most cherished option but rather than going into detail, she allowed me to phone her brother, who gasped when I told him the news. He said he was on his way.

We sat silently in the living room and although she offered us coffee, we both declined. The shock of her sister's death had robbed Meredith of her vitality. She had collapsed into herself and when her brother arrived, we made our introductions, expressed our condolences, and got out of there.

Buzz dropped me at my car. "I'll compile the history and cross-check it with the Julia Murphy crime book."

"You think we have a serial killer in our midst?"

"It's likely."

I shook my head. "You'll let me know what you find?"

"As soon as I have something."

"We're sure to be inundated by the media."

"We'll deal with it."

"Pressure."

"By the barrels full."

I nodded.

"Buddy?"

I looked at him.

"Don't let this get to you. It's all going to work out fine."

I watched him drive away.

"Says you," I muttered to myself.

SIXTEEN

"How's your shoulder?" my father asked.

We were on his back porch, dappled sunlight pouring through the trees accompanied by a breeze that rustled the branches and encouraged the myriad birds to outdo each other in cheerful song.

"Still sore, but better."

"How's the District Attorney?"

"Actually, Mr. Lytell has yet to speak directly to me, but his associate, Mr. Wilder, has advised me to hire counsel."

"Because of the Ivan's lawsuit?"

"Boris Petrov."

"Yeah. Him. Crummy Ivan. Friend of Putin, I hear."

"So rumor has it."

"Have you someone in mind?"

"I do."

"Who?"

"An L.A.-based lawyer. Someone that Petrov's team will know and respect."

"And you believe this person can stand up to anything Petrov might throw at him?"

"Her."

"You mean your lawyer's a her?"

"I do."

"A woman?"

"Try to keep your wits about you, Dad. Yes, she's a woman. And she's every bit the equal of Team Petrov. Better, in all likelihood."

"But a woman. Against all these heavy-hitters."

"Your misogyny is showing. Try to remember you're married to an attorney. A woman who also happens to be the Mayor of Freedom."

The Sheriff sat silently for a while, comfortable in our silence.

"What about this second killing?"

"Troublesome."

"What do you know?"

"It's what we don't know that's the most informative."

"Meaning?"

"Killer is experienced. He or she has managed to pull off a pair of brutal shootings without leaving even a trace of a clue. Same M.O. both times. Forensics identified each bullet as having been fired from a Walther PPS M2. I'm waiting for the next shoe to drop."

"You mean another killing."

I nodded.

"And you expect it to mirror the first two?"

"I do."

"And then what?"

"Good question."

"Is there a good answer?"

"None I could give you."

SEVENTEEN

We met for a late breakfast at The Original Pantry, the legendary downtown Los Angeles diner that has never shut its doors since it first opened in 1924. Its motto: *WE NEVER CLOSE.*

Jordyn Yates was already seated when I arrived and I spotted her before she saw me. I was once again bowled over by her striking beauty, a natural blue-eyed blonde in a navy Donna Karan suit, worn with an oversized, red polka-dotted necktie, clearly just for the fun of it.

She looked up as I approached and her face was instantly electrified by her joyful smile, the one that emphasized her prominent cheekbones and luscious lips, the smile I fell hard for the first time I saw it.

I leaned down to give her a peck on the cheek but she turned and planted an open-mouthed kiss full on my mouth and held it for a second or two longer than necessary. She broke into her throaty laugh when she noticed my discomfort.

"There's a Marriott next door, Buddy. What do you say?"

"Ha. Ha."

"What ha ha? I'm serious."

"I'll take a rain check."

"You don't know what you're missing."

"That's just the point. I do know."

I sat opposite her at a corner table. The normally bustling restaurant was enjoying a small respite between the breakfast rush and the onset of lunch. No sooner had I sat when a gnarly waiter appeared with two covered coffeepots, one in each hand.

"Hard or soft?"

"Hard."

"Mit or mit-out?"

"Mit-out, please."

He poured me a cup of regular and after offering Jordy a refill, which she declined, he spun on his heel and hurried off.

"How long has it been?" she asked.

"Three, four years maybe."

"Jesus, it goes fast."

"You married?"

"What are you, nuts? Are you?"

"You have to ask?"

"You never know. Age does strange things to people. Kids become a factor. Fear, too."

"Fear of?"

"Living alone for the rest of your life."

"Were you ever afraid of that?"

"Yeah, right."

We sat quietly for several moments.

"I didn't think for a minute you were married, Buddy."

"Why's that?"

"Weren't you the winner of the *NO COMMITMENTS MAN OF THE YEAR* Award?"

"I was. The same year you won the *NO COMMITMENTS WOMAN*. We each celebrated by going home with a stranger."

She threw back her head and emitted her deep, raspy laugh. "I'll do it," she said.

"Do what?"

"Whatever it is you want me to do. I miss you, Buddy. No matter what, we'll have a few laughs."

I told her what it was I wanted.

She flashed me her famous dead-eyed stare and lowered her voice. "Maybe I shouldn't have spoken so fast."

"It's a slam dunk."

"When it comes to the three idiots at Leonard, Howard and Arthur, it's a slam dunk. But this Petrov character dances only to his own music."

"Well he's cutting a rug with me. It was the DA who suggested I lawyer up."

"Well, consider yourself lawyered. And by the best in the business, I might add. I'll devote myself to seriously wounding this Russki son of a bitch."

"Thank you."

"Not so fast, big boy. There's the matter of a retainer to be discussed. I work for a large firm whose only yardstick is the size of its fees."

"Just send me a bill."

"Will I get dinner?"

"Yes."

"Will I get more than dinner?"

"Which means?"

"You know damn good and well what it means."

"Negatory."

"Oh, goody."

"What goody?"

"I love a challenge."

● ● ● ● ●

On the drive back to Freedom, my thoughts were of Jordyn Yates.

We met when I was summoned to testify in the trial of a noted gang leader whose arrest I had engineered. She was then a prosecutor attached to the Los Angeles County District Attorney's office. I was a street cop.

She had given me the once-over when I entered the courtroom and during her cross-examination of me, she exuded a kind of sexual subtext that caught my attention.

I had testified in the late afternoon, following which I had hung around outside the courtroom until the judge recessed for the day.

She saw me when she exited in the company of her two associates. She quickly ditched them and approached me.

"You're still here because?"

"I was hoping to get lucky."

"Arrogant little prick, aren't you?"

"Not so little."

"And you think you have a chance of getting lucky with me?"

"I do."

"Why?"

"I'm right, aren't I?"

"About what?"

"I am going to get lucky with you."

"Luck comes in many shapes and sizes, my friend."

"Your place or mine?"

"Mine," she said.

We were together for nearly a year.

Even though we were terrific together, we were each involved in the culture of noncommitment, more concerned with freedom than relationship. We often came close to professing our love for each other, but whenever the subject popped up, we always managed to skip out on it.

It was when she joined Thompson & McGill as a full partner that we drifted apart. I was in the process of becoming a homicide detective. She was busy proving to her partners and herself that she was worthy of partner status. One day I looked up and realized we hadn't seen each other in nearly three weeks.

We spent one final night doing all we could to avoid saying good-bye. But from that night to this day, we hadn't laid eyes on each other.

I knew instantly that the spark was still there. Truth be told, I would have gone to the Marriott with her in a New York minute. But I knew full well she was now my attorney and it would be a huge mistake to mess around with her.

"Don't shit where you eat," my father had so eloquently informed me any number of times.

This time I was determined to take his advice.

EIGHTEEN

I was heading north on 101 when the cell phone shattered my reverie. When I answered, I found Marsha Russo on the other end.

"Forewarned is forearmed," she said.

"Thank you. Was that all?"

"You wish."

"What is it?"

"There's a small contingent of unhappy citizens awaiting your arrival."

"You mean at the station?"

"It's amazing how fast you grasp these things, Buddy."

"You purposely set out to ring my chimes, didn't you, Marsha?"

"The beach is closed."

"I'm sorry?"

"The access points to the beach in front of Casa Petrov have been shuttered. The protesters came all the way from Los Angeles to spend the day on that particular stretch of beach. When they found each of the access points blocked by chain link fences topped with barbed wire, they called here. They're very angry."

"I'll have a look. Ask Johnny to meet me out there."

"What about the crowd?"

"Humor them. In your inimitable manner."

"Is that flattery or insult?"

"Figure it out for yourself."

I arrived at the beach road and made my way to the first of the access points. As Marsha claimed, a chain link fence had been erected at the spot where we had created an access. It was topped with dangerous threads of barbed wire. A bright red sign was hung on the fence exclaiming: *NO TRESPASSING.*

Johnny Kennerly arrived shortly after I did. Together we visited each of the four access points. Each of them was now fenced off.

"How could they do this?" Johnny asked.

"Beats me."

"Surely they can't expect to get away with it."

"You'd think."

"What do we do?"

"We get the BearCat out here and do it all over again."

● ● ● ● ●

The BearCat battering ram was accompanied by two Sheriff's cruisers, each containing four armed deputies.

We were all watching from the roadway in front of the original access point as the BearCat took down the chain link fence.

Once down, the ten protestors who had made their way from the station to the Petrov property, stepped onto the sand. All ten carried surfboards. Together with two of the deputies, they headed for the shoreline.

I heard the whine of the motorcycle engines before I actually saw them. They were revealed as they rounded the beach road bend and steamed in our direction. A pair of Harleys, each bearing a uniformed member of the Petrov security force.

They skidded to a stop in front of us and the lead goon jumped off of his bike, removed his helmet and approached me, a billy club in his hand. "What in the fuck you think you're doing?" he demanded.

I stared at him and said nothing.

"You're trespassing, is what you're doing. So scram. Now."

"I'm guessing you never saw the memo."

"Memo? What memo?"

"The one that says do as the Sheriff instructs you to do."

"There is no such memo," he said, angrily. "This here is private property. Sheriff or no Sheriff, you're still trespassing. Get out of here."

We stood face-to-face, close enough for me to notice the tufted black hairs that infested each of his flaring nostrils.

I found it hard to understand why all of these Russian security bozos thought it was in their interests to challenge the local law enforcement officials. I thought maybe they misunderstood me and my position because I wasn't wearing any kind of uniform.

I don't like uniforms, by the way. A by-product of a youth spent with a dictatorial father who enjoyed dressing me up in a miniature version of his Sheriff's uniform and parading me along with him to public events.

At one point, having heard *"Don't they look cute together?"* for what I deemed to be the last time, I took a pair of scissors to the damn thing and, with rare exceptions, never wore a uniform again.

It's a bone of contention between my father and me that I don't wear one now. I'm happy in jeans and a corduroy jacket. My uniform of choice. Which might be misleading to these Russian thugs.

But regardless of my dress code, surely they were aware of what happened to their associates. What would motivate the Petrov security forces to jeopardize their immigration status?

Is it possible they decided that working in a foreign country for a former KGB assassin was no longer beneficial to their health? That perhaps extradition was preferable to potentially deadly Petrov retribution for any perceived missteps?

Challenging us as they did would surely earn them a one-way

ticket back to Mother Russia. Perhaps they had come to believe they would be better served in Mother's care than in Father Petrov's.

Whatever their motivation, I thought it best to defuse this situation. "You're wrong about this. I think it would be in your best interests to clear out. Before you get yourselves into some serious trouble."

The biker had become increasingly more agitated. "I'm not going anywhere. I work here."

"Should I take that to mean you won't leave peaceably?"

"Take it as you want."

I turned to Johnny Kennerly. "Sheriff Kennerly, would you please read these two gentlemen their rights and then escort them to the county hoosegow?"

"It would be my pleasure."

Johnny and six of the other deputies surrounded the two bikers.

"Hands in the air," Johnny said.

The two Petrov employees stood staring at each other with a *what do we do now?* look.

Then the spokesman turned and made a move toward me. "To hell with you," he shouted, threatening me with his billy club.

I feinted left and kicked his legs out from under him. He dropped heavily to the ground.

I was on him in an instant. I wrested the billy club from his grasp and clubbed the back of his head with it. Then, using my forearm, I maneuvered him into a choke hold.

He was coughing violently when I secured both of his hands behind him.

When the coughing subsided, I got into his face. "You just made a big mistake, podner. Now it's going be my great pleasure to arrange for you and your pal over there to meet my friends at ICE. With any luck, you'll be on first plane to Moscow."

The man glared at me.

"Resist bail," I said to Johnny, who nodded.

After the two goons had been ushered away, we took down the new chain link fencing and loaded it onto a utility vehicle.

We left two of our deputies at the beach to make certain the surfers would be free of any further annoyances.

"Curiouser and curiouser," I mused.

NINETEEN

I parked my Wrangler in Shanghai Sam's parking lot. Visions of slippery shrimp and garlic string beans were crowding my mind when I spotted a sleek black Mercedes limousine heading swiftly in my direction.

I watched as it pulled up beside me and saw a malevolent-looking young man in a black suit exit the passenger side and approach me.

"Mr. Steel," he inquired in a thick Russian accent.

I looked at him.

He opened the rear door of the limo and motioned to me. "Mr. Petrov is requesting a word."

"In there?"

"He is in there, yes."

As I started for the car, the young man made a beckoning gesture. "Gun."

"Excuse me?"

"You have gun. Give to me."

"No."

The man took a step toward me. "Gun. Give me gun."

A voice from inside the limo bellowed, "Ivan. What's going on out there?"

The young man hollered, "He not give me gun."

"He wants to keep his gun?"

"*Da.*"

After several moments the voice said, "All right. Let him."

"Let him keep weapon?"

"I'll take my chances. It's all right, Mr. Steel," the voice proclaimed.

I stepped to the door and peered inside.

"The notorious Buddy Steel," Boris Petrov exclaimed. "Come sit with me for a few minutes. You'll be safe. I promise."

"And I can trust you because?"

"Because I say you can."

I shrugged and climbed inside. I sat on the jump seat across from him. The limo reeked of cologne. Middle-aged and impeccably dressed, the man extended his hand. "Boris Petrov."

I stared at him.

"I thought it was high time we made each other's acquaintance."

I shook his hand. "Mr. Petrov."

"Mr. Steel."

"How may I help you?"

"You've already helped me too much."

He spoke with only the trace of a Russian accent. He was short in stature, plain of feature, possessing the innate charm of a cobra. "I've been wracking my brain to come up with a good enough reason why you and I must remain on opposite sides. Forgive my presumptuousness, but allow me to present the facts as I understand them."

He looked at me as if seeking approbation.

"Go on."

"Thank you. My sources tell me you're not a long-timer here. You've come for familial reasons which are deemed to be short-lived. No insult intended."

"None taken."

"So I'd like to propose that for the purpose of this conversation, you give credence to the long haul."

"Meaning?"

He leaned forward. "We both know that this business with the Coastal Commission is rife with complexities. And without going into detail, allow me to suggest that these complexities can be resolved in very short order."

"How?"

"It's the age-old question. Who wouldn't be interested in becoming the beneficiary of a generous windfall?"

I stared at him blank-eyed.

"A windfall that would provide an economically sound future, one with no financial insecurities. Clear sailing, as they say, for the rest of one's life. How does that sound to you, Mr. Steel?"

"Like extortion."

"Oh, come on, Buddy. May I call you Buddy?"

Again I remained silent, fairly certain as to where this was headed.

"I'll deny having said it, but I'm offering you riches beyond your wildest imaginings. Say the word and within hours your life will have changed forever."

"And if I said no?"

"You'd lose my respect."

"Yikes."

"Don't sneer at this, Mr. Buddy. You'll never have such an opportunity again. Should you say no, you'll regret it for the rest of your life."

"It's not going to work, Boris. May I call you Boris?"

He scowled.

"If whatever it is you're doing here turns out to be criminal, you can bet your ass I'm going to find out exactly what it is and then provide you with a period of incarceration beyond your wildest imaginings. I'm not for sale."

Petrov shook his head. "You're making a big mistake."

"You think?"

"I know. Do reconsider the offer, Mr. Steel. There's still time to change your mind."

Without responding, I opened the car door.

The man in the black suit stood glaring as I exited the limousine. Once I was safely out, he got in and it sped away.

TWENTY

As I entered my office and dropped my stuff on the desk Marsha Russo meandered in and plunked herself down across from me.

"You're certainly Mr. Popularity this morning," she said with a smirk. She produced a handful of phone messages.

"Call out any name you think of and I'll match it with one of these babies."

"There's no need, Marsha. Just let me have the lot of them."

"Damn. I was sure you'd enjoy the game."

"You were wrong."

"Cranky, are we?"

Marsha had been part of the Sheriff's detail since even before my father's first term. She was a robust woman, possessing great energy, a *shtarker*, as the Sheriff was fond of calling her, quick-witted and brandishing an unnervingly smart mouth. I was her frequent target, which tickled me. She kept me and pretty much everyone else on our toes.

"May I please have the messages?"

She forked them over. "Best you start with Lytell and Wilder. They've been jumping out of their respective skins."

"Thank you."

"Shall I wait around? This promises to be very entertaining."

I glared at her.

"Okay, okay," she said as she stood up. "Deprive me of my pleasure. See if I care."

She closed the door behind her.

"It's about time," Skip Wilder said answering my call.

"What?"

"He's very concerned."

"The District Attorney?"

"Mr. Lytell, yes."

"Put him on."

"He's not here. And I'm not here, either. Are you in your office?"

"Yes."

"I'll call you back."

The call came after a ten-minute wait. "I'm outdoors. On a cell," Wilder said.

"Because?"

"Let's just say for a very good reason."

I let that sink in for several moments. Why would the Assistant District Attorney step outside and call me on his cell phone?

"If he's not there, I presume you're empowered to speak for Mr. Lytell."

"I am."

"Then speak."

"He's very concerned."

"You already said that.

"It required additional emphasis."

"Emphasis noted."

"This private property issue isn't going away. Craig Leonard is petitioning the California Superior Court. He's seeking an immediate injunction."

"Point him in the direction of James Morrison."

"He's gone."

"Who's gone?"

"Morrison. Left the job. Moved out of town. No forwarding address. Buh-bye."

"How could that be?"

"Off the record?"

I sighed."Okay."

"It appears as if a large chunk of money may have been dropped into the mix."

"Meaning?"

"Petrov may have proffered a very significant financial option that in the past always managed to catch the attention of the Coastal Commissioners."

"You think the Commissioners were bought off?"

"They have a history of it."

"I thought Morrison was brought in to put an end to the corruption."

"We all did."

"But?"

"He resigned and retired."

"And you think he caved?"

"Look, Buddy. We don't know what happened. But something other than everyday business came into play. Not only did Morrison resign, but the Coastal Commission did a sudden about-face regarding their consideration of Petrov's beach as a sanctuary. Why would they do that? Based on past performance, we suspect graft."

"A safe assumption."

"You think?"

"You're right about Petrov."

"Regarding the payoffs."

"Yes. Which is why you're outside on a cell phone."

"You can't be too cautious."

"What do you advise?"

"Off the record?"

"If you insist."

"I insist."

"Okay. Shoot."

"We believe Team Petrov is going to reconstruct the fence. Maybe it would be better to leave it alone this time."

"You mean allow closure of the access points?"

"Yes."

"No."

"What?"

"No. I won't leave it alone."

"You need to hear me, Buddy. You can no longer count on the support of the Coastal Commission. The Sheriff's Department is exposed. Best to leave it alone."

"Was there anything else?"

"Don't be goaded into making a mistake."

"It wouldn't be my first."

"There'll be reverberations."

"Then I'll wear anti-reverberation gear," I said and hung up.

I leaned back in my chair. "Petrov," I muttered to myself, "I guess he found a few takers."

TWENTY-ONE

"Your dime," Jordyn Yates said when she returned my call.

"And good day to you, too, Jordy."

"What's up, Buddy? I'm a busy girl, you know."

"Is the California Superior Court in your bailiwick?"

"You mean do I argue cases before it?"

"Yes."

"I do."

"Is it any fun?"

"What are you getting at?"

"Seems that Leonard, Howard and Arthur are arguing for injunctive relief from my having re-established public access points on the property owned by Boris Petrov. They're arguing that I interpreted the law incorrectly."

"Go on."

"Our Russian friend, Mr. Petrov, wants the fencing on his property restored and public beach access denied."

"And Craig Leonard is making a case for this to the Court?"

"Yes."

"And you want me to go up against him?"

"I do."

"What about the Coastal Commission?"

"You mean why aren't they taking the lead?"

"Something like that, yes."

"Looks as if the winds have shifted. The executive who was chosen to restore and uphold the Commission's integrity resigned and fled the state."

"Because?"

"Rumor is Petrov laid a bundle on them."

"You mean you think he paid off the Commissioners?"

"Wouldn't be the first time."

"And Leonard and Company?"

"I'm guessing their fees were significantly raised."

"So they're arguing a case on behalf of Petrov against a suddenly benign Coastal Commission."

"That's what I'm thinking."

"This isn't good, Buddy."

"Meaning?"

"Without the support of the Commission, you have no standing."

"Other than the marching orders I was originally given."

"I don't think they'll hold up. Particularly if the Commission has changed its tune."

"So, what do you advise?"

"Well, you could start by taking me to Cabo San Lucas for the weekend."

When I said nothing, she went on. "I don't think the judge will rule against Craig Leonard."

"Even if what he's arguing is wrongheaded?"

"Without the Commission's assent, yes."

"Shit."

"Cabo's looking better and better."

"If you went up against them, could you win any kind of a delay?"

"For what reason?"

"I don't know legally, but before they shut the door in my face, I'd love to investigate these alleged Petrov payoffs more closely.

This whole thing stinks. And I hate to think some Russian thug is buying his way out of it."

"Okay."

"Okay, what?"

"I'll see if I can stall things."

"What are the odds?"

"You mean for the average bozo lawyer or for me?"

"For you."

"You have to ask that? Really, Buddy?"

TWENTY-TWO

My father had summoned me and when I rang the doorbell, it was opened by my stepmother, the estimable Mayor Regina Goodnow.

"If there's even the slightest bit of poop anywhere, you're destined to step in it," she chided by way of welcome.

"I guess it's a good thing I'm not here to see you."

"Boris Petrov, Buddy? Really?"

I ignored her. "Where's Burton?"

"Why must you always be such an inveterate pot-stirrer?"

"I'll find him, Regina. Thanks just the same."

As I started toward the back of the house, she couldn't resist rubbing it in. "He needs this crap like a hole in the head."

I was feeling slightly sour this afternoon and it was an effort to stop myself from ringing her chimes. "Duly noted," I said, moving swiftly away.

The Sheriff was ensconced in his chair on the back porch, a gin and tonic sweating on the table in front of him. "Drink?"

"It's not that I don't want one," I commented as I sat down across from him.

"But?"

"Slurring my words is the last thing I need to be doing just now."

He grinned. It was clouding up in anticipation of late evening rain showers and the air was turning thick and muggy. A pair of crows were going at it in a neighboring tree, screaming at each other ceaselessly.

"Sounds like me and Regina," the old man quipped.

He was unusually cheerful. The experimental drug regimen was doing him good. "My phone hasn't stopped ringing," he added.

"And the consensus?"

"Mixed. A goodly number are known to curry Petrov's favor. The rest hate him."

"And the dividing line?"

"Those who receive and those who don't."

"Big surprise."

"For what it's worth, I think you're doing the right thing, Buddy. This *schmendrick* is as crooked as my late Uncle Herbert."

"Uncle Herbert was crooked?"

"Scoliosis."

"Very funny."

"Plus he's got allies."

"How many are Coastal Commissioners?"

"Good question. Enough to have faced down James Morrison, that's for sure."

"Why?"

"You mean why would they go up against Morrison?"

"Yes."

"Follow the money."

"Bribes?"

"Not in any traceable manner, but a credible source mentioned an unconscionable sum and suggested it was the basis of the Commission's sudden reconsideration of Petrov's property status."

"You mean the sanctuary status?"

"Bingo. Craig Leonard is readying a slate of environmental gurus who will testify that the sanctity of Petrov's beach property is essential for maintaining a valid coastal ecological support system."

"He made a run at me."

"Petrov?"

"Promised me riches beyond my imagination."

"And?"

"I accepted his offer and I just stopped in to say farewell. I've purchased a castle in the south of France and I can hardly wait to get there."

He glared at me. "Must you?"

I grinned at him. "What he did purchase was a group of ecological mercenaries who would slice up their own mothers if the price was right."

"It's good to be the king," the Sheriff said. "Except if there's someone around who's capable of de-throning you."

"Meaning?"

"Keep going, Buddy. Unleash Jordyn Yates. Call out the Commission. Make headlines. Challenge Craig Leonard. Sooner or later, just as in the past, the corruption will be revealed and a new slate of Commissioners will replace the old. And maybe then, just maybe, the payoffs will stop."

"Talk about an ideologue," I said.

"Old age and infirmity do that to you."

"Are you worried you'll be dragged into this?"

"I don't have any idealistic illusions, if that's what you're getting at. These bastards at Petrov's law firm will do everything they can to bring us both down. I say let 'em try."

"Even if it threatens to get uncomfortable for you?"

"Bring it on," he said.

TWENTY-THREE

"Leonard filed," Jordyn Yates announced when I picked up her call. "San Remo Superior Court."

"And?"

"I filed as well."

"So what happens now?"

"We go to court is what happens."

"When?"

"Soon. I'll let you know when I hear from the bailiff."

"I assume I can attend."

"Our case would be up shit's creek if you didn't."

"So, I'll take that as a yes."

"I knew there was a reason I'm so nuts for you, Buddy."

"I'll look forward to hearing from you."

"And seeing me, too." She ended the call.

I turned my chair to the window and sat back with my feet up. It was threatening rain and the sky was a mass of windblown dark clouds.

What little I knew about the San Remo Superior Court focused mostly on the judge, Her Honor Marielle Lemieux, a Freedom native and coincidentally, the mother of my high school sweetheart, Analiese Lemieux.

Small town.

Judge Lemieux had been a partner in a prominent San Remo-based law firm and was elected to her first six-year term on the bench when Analiese and I were dating. She was a prepossessing woman with a ready smile, quick wit, and, as a single parent, wary of me and my intentions regarding her daughter.

Now she, like my father, was just beginning a third term in office. A highly regarded justice, her responsibilities as the sole judge in a small county branch of the California Superior Court were wide-ranging and absolute.

I hadn't seen her in a number of years but when I joined the Sheriff's Department to assist my unwell father, one of the first congratulatory notes I received was from her.

My reverie turned to Analiese Lemieux, now a locally prominent attorney, wife, and mother. We were seventeen when we discovered each other. On the first day of the fall semester of our senior year. She was seated across the aisle from me in History class. She caught me staring at her. A quizzical look darkened her face.

She frowned. I smiled.

After class, I caught up with her in the hall. She was tall, athletic-looking, graceful. Mid-length layered copper blond hair haphazardly surrounded her angular face with its prominent cheekbones, celestial nose, sultry lips, and deep brown eyes. I was visibly smitten, which annoyed her.

"What?"

"Buddy. Buddy Steel."

"So?"

"Are you always this unfriendly?"

"Mostly."

"Okay. I just wanted to introduce myself."

"And now you have."

"Yes."

"Was there anything else?"

"Maybe."

"Like what?"

"Like, will you marry me?"

She stared at me for several moments, then walked away.

The next day I followed her again.

"Is this going to be a regular occurrence?"

"Probably. Yes."

"And if I object?"

"Without even giving me a chance?"

She sighed loudly and started to move off.

"After school," I shouted.

"What after school?"

"Meet me at the football field."

"Why would I do that?"

"Because you want to as much as I do."

She walked away without comment, but later, as I was sitting nervously in the bleachers, I spotted her heading in my direction. Soon thereafter, we were inseparable.

We confessed our love for each other, but stopped short of physically consummating it, which created a frustrating barrier between us that in the long run drove us apart.

In later years, when we caught up with each other during holidays or homecomings, we admitted how naive we had been. How frightened we were of sex and its potential impact on our lives.

In hindsight we acknowledged that while we shared a fervent attraction, and should have lovingly surrendered our respective virginities to each other, it wasn't fear of the sexual experience that prevented us from consummating our love. It was, rather, the dread of a first-love commitment from which neither of us believed we could escape unscathed.

Which laid the groundwork for what was to become the pattern of my life. Hooking up but not settling down. Commitment panic.

"What's so neurotic about that?" I was asking myself when the intercom buzzed me back to consciousness.

"Speak," I answered.

"Trouble," Wilma Hansen responded. "Line three."

"Buddy Steel," I said picking up the call.

"We got another one, Buddy," Buzz Farmer announced.

"Tell me."

"Same M.O. Downtown."

"Where?"

He told me.

"I'm on my way."

TWENTY-FOUR

The crime scene was on Market Street, located in the newly renovated part of downtown that had been designed to replicate what the area looked like at the turn of the twentieth century.

A tourist destination, the main part of the thoroughfare was closed to all but pedestrian traffic. Shoppers and tourists crowded the myriad restaurants and high-end boutiques that fronted the roadway.

A late-model silver Land Rover Discovery had just pulled out of a permissible parking space at the far end of the street when its driver, a stylishly dressed woman who appeared to be in her early forties, was shot to death through the driver's-side open window.

As was the case with the earlier killings, the inside of the Discovery was a bloody mess. There were no discernible clues.

Deputies Farmer and Striar were on the scene, their investigative process already underway. Norma Richard, the county coroner, had also arrived as had a forensics team and an ambulance, all of them hoping to avoid the approaching rain.

A tent had been set up across the street from where the murder occurred. Members of the press, including TV reporters and technicians, were setting up inside. One or two of the reporters shouted questions at me, but apart from offering them a friendly greeting, I ducked them.

Farmer and I studied the crime scene, walking the length and breadth of the area, hoping to discover anything that might aid in solving what was an increasingly alarming series of murders.

Farmer conducted himself with the confidence of someone whose past had been littered with random killings. While he paid lip service to the emotional impact of these tragedies, he appeared bereft of emotion. He walked through the investigations with self-possession and assertiveness, but also with an odd detachment that I found disquieting.

"What do you make of this, Buddy?" Buzz inquired.

"I wish I had something concrete to offer. What jumps out at me is the killer's expertise. These weren't just randomly chosen locations. As was the case with the first two, there are no security cameras here. Hence, we have no photographic information to assist us."

"So, what does that tell you?"

"That the killer was more concerned with finding the location than in choosing the victim. Our perpetrator is pretty crafty. He or she spends whatever time it takes to find an appropriate location and then, once selected, he or she stakes it out until the moment is exactly right. And, given the constraints of this particular location, finding the right combination of time and victim presented the killer with a singular challenge."

"You think it's like a game for him."

"Or her," I added. "I do. And it's a far more complicated game than what meets the eye. Pulling off murders of this kind without leaving even a shred of evidence is exceptionally difficult. We may be dealing with some kind of criminal mastermind here. These killings represent a deadly combination of impeccable planning and ingenious execution. No pun intended."

"So, how do we find this so-called mastermind?"

"Beats me."

"I'm serious, Buddy. How do we go about finding this person?"

"On a wing and a prayer?"

TWENTY-FIVE

"It's bothering me," I said to Marsha Russo.

We were sitting in my office, listening to the rain as it pelted the windowpane, the storm having already reached its peak, diminishing now as it moved south.

"What is?"

"There's something about these murders that keeps gnawing at me. Maybe it's their meticulousness. The huge amount of planning in order for the conditions to be just right."

"So?"

"I don't know, Marsha. It rankles. It feels…I don't quite know how to say it cohesively…it feels like the killer has been doing this for a while. A number of times. My gut tells me it's less about the actual killings and more about the fastidiousness of the crimes. Does that make any sense?"

"Go on."

I stood and began mindlessly pacing the office. "Let's assume the perp has satisfied his need to kill. We know he's done it before. But what if he didn't totally appease his psychotic needs? What if he's now raising the stakes of the game."

"The game?"

"Forgive me for using that term. But in truth, it feels to me as if, with regards to this particular killer, it is a game. I believe it's less about the need to kill and more about the logistics. A psychotic need to commit the perfect crime. Repeatedly."

I sat back down and listened to the rain for a while. "Let's assume you're right," Marsha said. "How do you go about solving it?"

"Good question."

"And the answer?"

"Are you up for some added responsibility?"

"Who, me?"

"Of course you. Who else am I talking to?"

"What kind of added responsibility?"

"Legwork."

"What legwork?"

"Helping me find the killer."

"You know something, Buddy? You're very skilled at talking in circles."

"Thank you."

"I didn't mean that as a compliment."

"So, what's your answer?"

"My answer to what?"

"Doing legwork."

"What exactly is it you want me to do?"

"Make use of your exceptional technological skills."

"Flattery will get you nowhere, Buddy."

"Listen to me, Marsha. If I'm right, this killer has a history. Somewhere out there are a number of unsolved, serial-style murders. They could be anywhere. I want you to research and locate these unsolveds and see if we can find any kind of pattern that fits the profile of our guy."

"Or girl."

"Her, too."

Marsha sat silently for several moments. Then she said, "I can do that."

"There's every chance it will be time-consuming and possibly even fruitless."

"I'll still do it."

"Why?"

"I don't know, Buddy. It certainly isn't out of any measure of devotion or kiss-ass need to please you."

"How depressing."

"But I like your train of thought."

"And?"

"I'm a glutton for punishment." Marsha stood and headed for the door.

I stopped her. "One thing more."

"It's always something."

"Let's keep this to ourselves."

"Meaning?"

"Just that. Only you and I can know about it."

"Why?"

"Call it my coply intuition."

"Which means?"

"I wish I knew."

TWENTY-SIX

The hearing was to take place in the San Remo County Court-house.

When I arrived, I spotted a larger than usual crowd assembled outside. The press contingent stood in a roped-off section along with a number of local TV reporters and their crews.

I stepped quickly through the melee and was on the court-house steps when one of the reporters recognized me and began firing questions.

"Do you have any suspects in the killings?"

"Are you going to hold strong on the beach access issue?"

"Where's the Sheriff and why isn't he in charge?"

I slipped inside the courthouse without answering and took a moment to gather myself. Then I entered the courtroom and found a seat at the back of the amply filled gallery.

A handsomely dressed, middle-aged man was standing in front of the witness stand questioning a nerdy-looking man while Marielle Lemieux, in her judge's robes, sat at the bench intently listening.

I presumed the questioner was Craig Leonard, the lead attorney of Boris Petrov's legal team.

Jordyn Yates sat alone at the defense table. At one point, when she looked around to check out the attendees, we made eye contact. She winked at me.

Leonard finished questioning the nerdy young man, then called a solemn-looking, thirty-something woman to the stand. Prior to her being sworn in, Judge Lemieux motioned for Leonard to step to the bench.

I could barely make out their conversation but it appeared he was indicating this would be the prosecution's last witness.

The judge nodded and Leonard went on to ask the woman a series of questions relating to bird species and their sanctuaries. When Leonard seemed satisfied with her testimony, he thanked the witness and said, "No more questions, Your Honor."

Judge Lemieux turned to Jordyn, who waived any cross-examination. Then, in answer to the judge's question, she said, "Just one witness, Your Honor."

"Please proceed."

Jordyn called me and as I made my way to the witness stand, Judge Lemieux made eye contact with me and despite herself, broke into a large grin.

Once I was sworn in, Jordyn asked, "What is your association with Boris Petrov?"

"Very little, actually. I've only met him once."

"But you've had some interaction with his staff."

"Yes. The San Remo Sheriff's Department was empowered by the California Coastal Commission to enforce the beach access laws as they pertained to Boris Petrov's property."

"And what exactly did that entail?"

"The removal of permanent fencing that had been constructed at the four access points which had previously afforded beach-goers a right-of-way."

"Did you meet with any resistance to this undertaking?"

"A handful of Petrov's goons accosted me and my deputies on two different occasions."

Craig Leonard stood and averred. "We object to the term *goons*, Your Honor."

"Sustained," the judge said. "Please find different nomenclature for Mr. Petrov's employees."

I nodded and smiled.

"And what were those occasions?" Jordyn asked.

"Once, when we were bulldozing the permanent fencing that was then blocking a previous access point. And again as we were removing the new fencing that Petrov's goons...uh, I'm sorry, Petrov's men...had constructed elsewhere to prevent public ingress to the beach."

"And how exactly were you accosted?"

"The first time was just after we had successfully restored an original access point. One of the Petrov thugs shoved me and their leader, a Mr. Volya Koskoff, made a menacing gesture toward me."

Leonard stood and said, "We object to the word *thug*."

"Sustained," Judge Lemieux said. "Sheriff Steel?"

"I apologize, Your Honor. These Petrov employees behaved like thugs."

"Objection," Leonard said.

"Overruled."

Jordyn seized the moment and quickly went on. "What was your response to this so-called thuggish behavior?"

"One of my deputies tasered them both."

"And the result of the tasering?"

"Wet undies and jail time."

Judge Lemieux could barely stifle her laughter.

"Objection," Leonard shouted. "These men are highly trained members of Boris Petrov's security task force."

"And illegal immigrants, as well," Jordyn said.

"Objection," Leonard said.

The judge turned to him. "To your knowledge, Mr. Leonard, are either of these assailants in the country illegally?"

"It's possible," Leonard said sheepishly.

"Possible?"

"They're in custody until such time as that determination is made."

"Objection overruled," Judge Lemieux said.

Leonard sat down heavily, muttering something unintelligible under his breath.

"Excuse me," the judge said. "I didn't quite hear you."

"Nothing, Your Honor."

"I should hope so," she said sternly.

"And the second assault…?" Jordyn asked me.

"It was at the same location. We were confronted by another pair of Petrov's…employees. We were in the process of tearing down the new fencing they had just finished erecting when one of them attacked me physically."

"And?"

"I put him down."

"You did what?"

"I immobilized him."

"How?"

"Superior martial arts training."

"Yours?"

"Yes."

"And what happened then?"

"The men were arrested and are currently being held without bail awaiting a deportation hearing."

"I'm led to believe there was another incident," Jordyn said.

"There was."

"Can you describe it?"

"I was attacked from behind by another of Mr. Petrov's security officers. He struck me twice with a tire iron."

"And?"

"I shot him."

"You shot the Petrov employee?"

"In the hip."

"Objection," Craig Leonard protested.

"What is the objection this time?" the judge asked.

"We don't deny the fact that Mr. Steel was assaulted by a member of the Petrov security contingent. But we want to go on record as to Mr. Petrov's involvement in this attack. He steadfastly denies any knowledge of or participation in this event. He apologizes for the unsanctioned behavior of one of his employees."

"Duly noted," Judge Lemieux stated.

Jordyn addressed the judge. "No further questions, Your Honor."

Judge Lemieux turned to Craig Leonard. "Any questions?"

"Yes, Your Honor."

He approached the witness stand and stood directly in front of me. "You referred to Mr. Petrov's staff as…let me get this straight…*goons* and *thugs*."

"I did."

"Because?"

"Because that's what they are."

"For the record, that's your personal opinion."

"Correct."

"They're actually top-notch, highly qualified security personnel."

"That's your opinion."

"Correct," Leonard said.

"But if the laws of the land are upheld, these *qualified security personnel* will soon be on their way back to the cesspool of a country they crawled out of."

Leonard turned to the judge. "As you can see, Your Honor, this witness has no respect for Mr. Petrov's security detail nor their place of birth. As a result, his credibility should be discounted."

"Thank you for your opinion, Mr. Leonard," Judge Lemieux said.

Leonard nodded. "Thank you, Your Honor. No further questions."

After I was dismissed, I returned to my seat at the back of the courtroom. The judge had summoned both attorneys to the bench and they were engaged in a three-way conversation.

When they finished, Judge Lemieux banged her gavel loudly. "Injunction denied," she said.

Then she headed for her chambers.

I made my way to Jordyn, who greeted me with a warm smile.

"Congrats," I said.

"Aw, shucks," she chided. "The judge asked if you might stop by her chambers."

I nodded.

"Forgive me," Jordyn said.

"For what?"

"I have to scoot back to L.A."

"You mean now?"

"Tragic, isn't it?"

"You mean before…?"

"There's no need to belabor the point, Buddy. I get it."

She stepped up to me and kissed me quickly. She searched my eyes. "I can hardly wait for this dinner of ours."

I smiled. "Me, too."

"Liar."

TWENTY-SEVEN

The door to her chambers was opened by Judge Marielle Lemieux's bailiff, who held her finger to her lips and pointed to the judge who was at her desk, engaged in what appeared to be a lively conversation with Craig Leonard.

When she spotted me, Judge Lemieux excused herself to Leonard, then stood and approached me. After a warm hug, she led me to a small sitting area. "I'm sorry about this, Buddy. He asked to see me and now I'm stuck with him."

"Not to worry. You do look a bit frazzled. Are you okay?"

"Oh, yes. It's nothing. But I didn't want to let the chance to give you a hug pass without its fulfillment."

"How's Analiese?"

"And her three children."

"Three?"

"Two girls and one lunatic."

"Do I detect a sexist attitude here?"

"Wait until you meet him before you head down that road. He's three, he never stops talking, his sisters are terrified of him, and I'm embarrassed to add that so is his mother. Have you ever heard the expression *Holy Terror?*"

"And he's the one you love best?"

"How did you know?"

"Because in some circles, you're referred to as a Holy Terror yourself."

"*Moi?*"

From her desk, Craig Leonard emitted a loud, theatrical cough.

"Duty calls," the judge said.

"It's always a treat to see you."

"You realize that were it not for your own lunacy, I'd now be your mother-in-law."

"Lunacy?"

"You're still unmarried, am I right?"

"Yes."

"Determinedly so, right?"

"I guess you could say that."

"I rest my case."

"You know what the only thing was that frightened me more than marriage to Analiese?"

"No. What?"

"Having you as a mother-in-law."

She swatted at me, a big grin breaking out on her face. "You should only be so lucky. Now get out of here. Can't you see how busy I am?"

• • ● • •

No sooner had I gotten into the Wrangler than my cell phone started ringing.

"Buddy Steel," I answered.

"Sheriff Steel?" a woman's voice asked.

"Who wants to know?"

"Wendy Kassel. You may not remember me, but I work for James Morrison. The Coastal Commissioner. Or should I say '*worked for him.*' We met once when you were in the building."

"What can I do for you, Ms. Kassel?"

"I suppose you know about James."

"I know he's no longer a Coastal Commissioner."

"Do you know why?"

"Only the rumors."

"I'm not supposed to be talking to you."

"Because?"

"I've been warned not to."

"Warned?"

"You have no idea as to what happened, do you?"

"I'm guessing I don't."

"Things aren't as they appear. James has gone into hiding. I'm about to follow."

"What is it you're saying?"

"Commissioner Morrison's resignation was influenced."

"By money, I heard."

"You seriously believe James Morrison accepted a bribe?"

"That's the rumor."

"It wasn't money that influenced him."

"What, then?"

"They broke both of his thumbs."

"Excuse me?"

"Two Russian men went to his home. They gave him a choice."

"Choice being?"

"Disappear or suffer the consequences."

"Which were?"

"I'll leave that to your imagination. Breaking his thumbs was for openers."

"You're suggesting that Boris Petrov's men scared him off."

"So much so that he was gone in a day and no one knows where he went."

"How do you know this?"

"Because he phoned me from the road and suggested I do the same."

"Leave town?"

"And go into hiding."

"And he suggested this because?"

"Maybe you're not as smart as he gave you credit for. I worked with Jimmy for years. I know what really went down. And that knowledge has put me in danger. So I'm forced to leave. Please don't try to find me."

She ended the call.

I pulled onto the shoulder of the road and sat quietly for a while, contemplating what I'd just learned.

James Morrison had been scared off. Because he wouldn't accept a bribe. And as a result of his refusal, he suffered a brutal consequence. KGB tactics. As administered by Petrov's tortuous thugs.

Clearly, the stakes were higher than I had imagined.

Greater than just restricting access. What, though? What could be so important that Petrov is willing to resort to violence to keep it under wraps?

What's really going on with him?

TWENTY-EIGHT

"They broke his thumbs?"

"That's what she said."

"Ouch. Talk about painful."

My father and I were having lunch out, a rare experience for him these days. But he was feeling better, so he suggested it.

"What the hell," he had said, "why not?"

He had chosen The Freedom Country Club and its casual, members-only dining room overlooking the first hole of the Arnold Palmer-designed golf course.

He was heartened by the number of fellow members who stopped by our table to offer him their best wishes, many of them enjoying the chance to needle him, as well.

He was a popular figure in Freedom, known for paying heed to the less fortunate as well as those in the chips. He had once dreamed of the governorship and when he found that calling elusive, he started dreaming of it for me. Even when I was inching toward becoming an LAPD homicide detective.

Despite my resistance, he believed that by dint of his personality, he could persuade me to seek the office. He'd phone me regularly with campaign ideas. Slogans, even.

For a while I let him believe I was taking it seriously by way of ameliorating him. When I finally admitted I had no wish to run, it angered him.

For several months he churlishly referred to me as Governor Steel. As in, "How would the Governor like his eggs this morning?" Or, "When is the Governor planning on visiting his family?"

When he realized he had succeeded only in deepening the chasm between us, he reluctantly relented. I wondered if he would ever come to accept me for who I am.

The answer to which is why I'm currently in Freedom. Hopeful but wary.

"Something's rotten in Denmark," I said when things had quieted down."This Petrov thing has spiraled into a much bigger deal."

"Meaning?"

"That's just it. I don't know what it means."

"What are you thinking?"

"I'd like to have another chat with Vlad Smernik."

"He being?"

"One of the Petrov goons who threatened me."

"What good would that do?"

"He offered to provide information."

"Boris Petrov information?"

"Yes. He said there was more there than meets the eye."

"Which means?"

"I'm thinking it means there's something questionable taking place on his property that Petrov doesn't want anyone to know about. Otherwise, why would he maintain such a sizable security staff? What's so important that he needs that many guards? It's not like he's on the outs with the Kremlin and he's afraid Putin's going to poison him. He's a loyalist. So what's he hiding? Why is he so intent upon sealing off public access? What's going on there?"

"And you think this Smernik character is prepared to tell you about it?"

"Can't hurt to find out."

"Where is he?"

"Likely in an ICE holding pen."

"In Los Angeles?"

"Yes."

"And you think he's a horse trader?"

"Possibly."

"What have you got to trade?"

"His freedom."

"How would you arrange that?"

"I wouldn't. You would."

"Me?"

"You're the Sheriff."

"Hold on a second here, Governor. Don't be thinking I can help you arrange for this Russki to skate."

"If the information he delivers is useful enough, you can and will."

"You give me way too much credit."

"Don't go all self-deprecating on me, Burton. If this guy provides a leg up on a possible prosecution of Boris Petrov, there's no one better at negotiating a Get Out of Jail Free card than you."

"That's what you say."

"That's what everyone says."

TWENTY-NINE

Once she saw I was off the phone, Marsha Russo sauntered into my office and sat across from me.

"Breaking news," she announced.

"Hit me."

"He's in the Metropolitan Detention Center on Alameda Street in downtown Los Angeles."

"I know it well."

"From which perspective?"

"Funny. How would you feel about setting up an appointment for me?"

"Business or social?"

"What difference would it make?"

"I don't do social."

"It's business."

"How do I know?"

"Because I want to meet privately with an inmate at the detention center."

"Male or female?"

"What difference does that make?"

"I wouldn't want to be involved in any conjugal thing."

"You know, Marsha, sometimes you can be a royal pain in the ass."

"I know. It's in my gene pool."

"Vlad Smernik."

"He's who you want to meet with?"

"Yes. And it has to be private. Outdoors, preferably. No bugs. No hovering supervision. You'll need to arrange it with Captain Rodger Pike."

"When for?"

"Tomorrow morning, if possible."

She stood and lumbered toward the door. "I'm on it."

I called out to her. "What's up with the other thing?"

"I'm on it, too."

"And?"

"I'm weeding stuff out."

"Meaning?"

"You have no idea how many unsolved homicides there are. I've narrowed the search to serials but even at that, it's a ball breaker."

"How soon?"

"Soon enough. I'm getting warmer. It's a good thing I like you, Buddy."

"Because?"

"It serves as a reminder as to why I'm doing this."

"Cheese?"

"Excuse me?"

"Would you like some cheese with that whine?"

She stared at me for several moments, then turned to leave. At the door, she chided me over her shoulder, "Not even remotely funny."

THIRTY

Captain Rodger Pike was homegrown, having risen in the ranks from his beginnings as a street cop nearly two decades ago.

His was a measured ascendency, one rank at a time, his experience gathered in a multitude of precincts located in a plethora of districts. When he reached Parker Center, then the LAPD headquarters, he was a seasoned veteran and an accomplished leader.

Now on the command staff, ensconced in the new Police Administration Building on First Street in downtown L.A., he was frequently mentioned as a potential candidate for Commissioner.

He stood when I entered his office and uncharacteristically, wrapped me in a bear hug and slapped me heartily on the back.

"You're a sight for sore eyes, Buddy."

"Rubbing the blarney stone this morning, are we, sir?"

"We miss you around here."

"That's very kind of you to say. Thank you."

He pointed me to the conference table located in a corner of his spacious office, overlooking the downtown corridor and the westside beyond it.

"So," he said once we were seated. "Are you liking it up there?"

"It's a challenge."

"But are you liking it?"

"Some days, perhaps. It's a small town freighted with small-town politics."

"The welcome mat is always out for you here, Buddy."

"Be careful what you wish for."

He smiled. "We've set up the meeting with this Smernik character. What is it you want from him?"

"You've heard of Boris Petrov?"

"Only what I read in the papers."

"He's violated the Coastal Commission rules regarding beach access, and the San Remo Sheriff's Department has been assigned the task of straightening him out."

"And?"

"He's defiant. He's thrown up every conceivable roadblock. Far greater than you can imagine. Actions above and beyond the norm."

"Which raised your hackles, no doubt."

"No doubt. The point is not so much his desire to maintain privacy. That's no different from any of these other self-entitled beachfront billionaires who do the same. But this guy is over the top. Way beyond the pale. Which makes me wonder what's really going on. What's he hiding?"

"Hence, Smernik."

"He was sent to deliver me a message. Rough me up a little. Warn me off. He and another goon. A pair of inept bozos in over their heads."

"So?"

"When I subdued him and we were waiting for the backup to arrive, he volunteered to share information with me regarding Petrov's activities."

"In exchange for his freedom, I'll bet."

"Yes."

"So you're here on a fishing expedition."

"I am."

"Well, it's set up as you requested. No one will be any the wiser. Hopefully, you can wrestle something worthwhile out of him."

"Not likely, but it's worth the effort. Many thanks for your help, sir."

"You'll let me know how you fare?"

"Be my pleasure."

THIRTY-ONE

I hoofed it to Alameda Street and the Metropolitan Detention Center where I was greeted by Sergeant Tony Ciavatta, himself a crusty relic of the department of yore.

"Where you keepin' yourself these days, Buddy?" he inquired.

"Freedom."

"A place or a state of mind?"

"Both."

"Well, you're lookin' fine, that's for sure."

"Not as fine as you, Tony."

"Still the bullshitter, eh, Buddy?"

"Takes one to know one."

He laughed and led me to the offices of the chaplain, where he ushered me into a tiny reflective garden where I found Vlad Smernik. The security guard assigned to watch over him nodded to me and stepped inside. "I'll be on the other side of the door," he said.

Smernik stared at me as if he were trying to remember exactly who I was. He was sitting on a bench next to a gurgling fountain, designed to override the sounds of the city and private conversations. Limestone pavers were scattered amid green St. Augustine grass. Christmas cactus and philodendron blossomed in large ceramic planters. Brick walls were overrun with abundant English ivy. The effect of the small garden was calming and peaceful.

"I know you," Smernik said.

"Buddy Steel."

"The guy who busted me in San Remo?"

"One and the same."

"What are you doing here?"

Smernik was dressed in an orange jumpsuit and his hands were cuffed behind his back. He appeared tired, dispirited, forlorn.

"You made me a proposition."

"So?"

"Perhaps I'll take you up on it."

"Perhaps? What perhaps?"

"You provide information I find helpful, I'll see about getting you out of here."

"You mean you pay after you eat?"

"Something like that. Yes."

"No deal."

"You have anything better?"

"What's to prevent you from just walking away?"

"Nothing."

"So why should I sing for you?"

"Listen to me, Vlad. I'm your only ticket out of here. You give me what I need, your ticket gets punched. You'll have to trust that I'll do what I say I'll do."

He stared at me. "What do you want to know?"

"Everything there is to know about Boris Petrov."

He sat silently for several moments. Then he said, "There's a drug lab on the property."

"Go on."

"He's got chemists working there. They invented some kind of synthetic substance not dissimilar to Fentanyl, and they're manufacturing it in large quantities."

"The opioid."

"A variant of it. Lethal. Some guy sampled it out there and didn't live to tell about it."

"What does he do with it?"

"Boats come to take it away."

"Boats?"

"Speedboats. Every week. They load up and ship out."

"Going where?"

"I wouldn't know. I only know about the manufacturing because a friend of mine from St. Petersburg is involved with the shipping part. Schmuck. He's so filled with himself that he couldn't help but brag about it."

"About his involvement with the opioid shipments?"

"Yes."

"Where's the lab?"

"Somewhere inside the mansion. It's a huge place, you know. There's plenty of room for it."

"This is very helpful, Vlad."

"So am I free to go?"

"Not yet. But you will be."

"Why not yet?"

"Verification."

"And?"

"Arrangements have to be made."

"So this was all bullshit."

"It was if that's what you want to believe."

"I want to believe I'm getting out of here."

"Listen to me, Vlad. It's not only a question of getting you out of here, it's also providing for your safety. If anyone were to find out it was you who ratted Petrov out, your life wouldn't be worth a plugged nickel. Relax. It might take me a few days to make all of the necessary arrangements."

"What if they deport me before you do?"

"They won't."

"And I should believe you because?"

"Let's not do this dance again. I'm on it. You'll just have to trust me."

"Trust. Hah. Trust an American cop? I feel like I've been sucker-punched."

I summoned the security guard who immediately entered the sanctuary. "Be nice to him."

"I'm nice to everyone," he said, a big grin spreading across his gnarled face.

"Why do I have trouble believing that?"

"Ye of little faith."

THIRTY-TWO

"What if his information is incorrect?"

"We can always rescind."

"So I'm sticking my neck out without proof positive."

"Look, Dad, proof positive or not, I believe the guy. Now I understand the subtext."

"What's that supposed to mean?"

We were in his office at the County Courthouse. His spirits were high. He had taken to putting time in at the office every few days or so. He didn't do a whole lot other than sit around and swap stories with the staff. Mostly his stories.

He made every effort to maintain the illusion that his health was improving, but occasionally he slipped up and opened the window to a crack in his armor.

My sister, Sandra, and her six-year-old daughter, Savannah, had recently come west for a weekend with the old man. Never a big fan of children, our father nevertheless made all the right noises regarding his love for the girl. He went so far as to play cards with her. Even read to her.

But when Savannah threw one of her legendary tantrums, it rankled him. Unable to calm her, he lost it himself. He yelled, which scared the daylights out of her. He raised his hand as if to hit her.

She glared at him and between tears, screamed, "I hate you. You're a mean old man. I want to go home."

To her mother who, along with our stepmother, Regina, had raced to her side, Savannah kept right on screaming. It took every ounce of Sandra's patience to calm her.

By the time she did, my father had long since fled the scene and had locked himself in his bedroom. "I don't know what came over me, Buddy," he exclaimed solemnly. "It's this fucking illness. I'm not myself."

"It's all right, Dad. She'll get over it."

"Yes, but will I?" he lamented.

"If Smernik is right," I said. "We're dealing with a federal offense."

"For which you'll need to involve the FBI."

"Ultimately."

"What more do you need?"

"Proof."

I stood and began pacing his oversized office with its floor-to-ceiling steel and glass windows that offered views of Freedom Township, the Santa Ynez Mountains to the north and the glistening Pacific to the west.

"I'm uncertain," I said.

"About?"

"How to verify Smernik's claim. Which we need to do before summoning the cavalry. "

"The choices?"

"A flat-out raid on the mansion."

"In search of the so-called fentanyl lab."

"Yes."

"And choice B."

"We lay in wait for the arrival of the boats."

"And catch them dead to rights loading the shit onto them."

"Something like that."

"Which do you prefer?"

"Would that I knew."

"You in the market for a little advice?"

"Why do you think I'm here?"

"At first I thought you might want to hear a few of my stories."

"I'd sooner sit through every Matthew McConaughey movie."

"Do what you think is best."

"That's the advice?"

"And rendered free of charge."

I stared at him. "That's what you would do?"

He thought for several moments."Likely, I'd prepare to do both."

"Both at the same time?"

"Yes."

"What would be the deciding factor?"

"Resistance."

"From Petrov's troops?"

"Yes."

"So where would you start?"

"Wherever the odds were in my favor."

"And you'd decide that when?"

"When I knew for certain that the boats would arrive."

"You mean you'd wait it out."

"Yes."

"And then decide."

"Yes," the Sheriff said. "And keep in mind that however it goes down, it's going to be a bitch."

"But you think it's the right thing to do?"

"One way or the other."

"Meaning?"

"Look, it's your deal, Buddy. You own it. But it's dicey. This so-called Fentanyl lab might not exist at all. Or it could be dismantled in an instant. Until you actually eyeball it, it's nothing more than the word of a snitch who's seeking asylum. You can't really tip your hand regarding the boats. You can't put an armada in their way. They'd freak and be gone in an instant.

"So there's very little to work with here. I suppose you could share the info with the FBI, but with no proof, there's the distinct possibility you could be standing alone with your dick in your hand. There's nothing easy or predictable in this. You're forced to take your chances. You make the first move and pray it's the right one."

"Or?"

"You take a victory lap regarding the right of access issue."

"And?"

"You look the other way."

"Meaning I leave them alone to carry on whatever subterfuge it is they're practicing."

"Yes."

"I can't do that."

"So, then, you mount your challenge, you catch them by surprise, and with luck, you take the whole operation down."

"So in other words, do what I think is best."

"Which is one fine piece of excellent advice, if I say so myself."

THIRTY-THREE

"Why, if it isn't Mr. Heavily in Demand himself," Marsha Russo exclaimed when I arrived at the office.

She quickly followed me inside. "Your call list is so massive I was unable to lift it."

"I'm in no mood, Marsha."

"Well, excuuuuse me. You have a great many calls."

"Starting with?"

"Messrs Lytell and Wilder, of course."

"Of course. May I ask you a question?"

"A question you need permission to ask?"

"Yes."

"I'm not liking the sound of this, but go on."

"Is there any fresh coffee?"

"I seriously doubt it."

I sat quietly.

"Well," Marsha said and made as if to stand. "If there's nothing else…"

"You wouldn't be willing to make a pot, would you?"

"Not likely."

"Even if you knew it would mean a great deal to me?"

She stood. "I'd have to take it under advisement."

"Marsha?"

"Okay. Okay."

"May I take that as a yes?"

She headed for the door. "We'll know soon enough, won't we?" she said and left.

"It's never easy," I muttered to myself.

"You'll have to hold on while I find Lytell," Skip Wilder said when he picked up my call. "I'll be right back." He put me on hold.

The music was some kind of melody-free annoyance that kept on repeating itself, a headache-inducing series of improvisational instrumental riffs that made water boarding seem like a reasonable alternative.

"I found him," Wilder said putting an end to the music. "We're just trying to figure out how to conference him in."

"You don't know how to mastermind a conference call?"

"The phones are new. It'll only take a second."

The music resumed and after about thirty seconds of it, I hung up.

I turned my chair so as to look out the window. I was greeted by a deep blue cloudless vista that made me think I was gazing into infinity.

"*Los dos homunculai* on line three," Wilma Hansen announced over the intercom. "One of them's whining about a dropped call."

"I hung up on them."

"You hung up on the District Attorney?"

"Yes."

"Wow. Two gold stars for you. Line three."

"You hung up, didn't you?" Wilder said.

"Not at all. The call was disconnected."

"You hung up."

"Boys, boys," District Attorney Michael Lytell interjected. "Is that you, Buddy?"

"Sir," I said.

"You've attracted a great deal of attention around here."

I remained silent.

"He hung up again," Wilder proclaimed.

"I didn't hang up."

"He didn't hang up," Lytell said. "He's still there. Listen, Buddy, I've already heard from the State's Attorney and from Boris Petrov's attorney."

"Good things, I hope."

"Don't mouth wise with me. It seems your friend Petrov, while petitioning for some kind of diplomatic status, claims he's being harassed by you."

"Diplomatic status?"

"He's dropping Vladimir Putin's name. Threatening to sic him on the Governor."

"To what end?"

"He's pissed his injunction was denied. Says it was a setup. He maintains he was protecting a wildlife sanctuary when he sealed off the access points. He blames you for instigating the ICE roundup of nearly his entire security force."

"He's pissed I wouldn't take his bribe. And he's lying about the wildlife preserve. And every one of the men we busted is working in the country illegally."

"Be that as it may, he's stirring the pot and making life difficult for us."

"What is it you're suggesting, Mike?"

"Stand down, Buddy. Leave the son of a bitch alone."

"No."

"Excuse me?"

"No. I'm not going to stand down."

"Did you hear that?" Lytell said to Wilder. "He says he's not going to stand down."

"Not a good idea, Buddy," Wilder said.

"I thank you both for your valued opinions. They don't hold much water for me, however."

"Maybe you didn't hear me too clearly," Lytell said. "I'm advising you to step away, Buddy."

"Thank you. I promise to seriously consider your advice."

Then I hung up.

After several moments, Wilma buzzed once more. "It's the Gold Dust Twins again."

"I'm not here."

"Excuse me?"

"Tell the District Attorney I was late for a meeting and ran out of the office."

"You want me to lie for you, is that what's happening, Buddy?"

"Can it, Wilma. Just do it."

"Roger. Wilco," she said.

Again I sat back in my chair. Marsha entered and placed a steaming cup of black coffee on my desk.

"You can't hardly know how important this is to me," I said taking a sip. "Thank you."

"You owe me big-time," she said and left.

The intercom rang again. "I said I wasn't here."

"Jordyn Yates on one," Wilma said. "Should I kiss her off, too?"

"No. No. I'll take it."

"Line one. The line with the flashing red light."

"Jordy?"

"One moment for Ms. Yates," a female voice said.

"Buddy?" Jordyn said when she picked up the call.

"Hi."

"It's amazing how you manage to wind up in the middle of as many shit storms as you do."

"What now?"

"Lieutenant Governor Lincoln Brady. United States Attorney Michael Kurtz. Craig Leonard of the illustrious law firm, Leonard, Howard and Arthur. Let's see, am I forgetting anyone?"

"What is it you're saying, Jordy?"

"They're gunning for you."

"So?"

"It's going to get hotter, too. Brady and Kurtz have petitioned the County regarding your status in the Sheriff's Department. They want you removed from office and they want to meet with your father to determine his ability to serve."

"This is all Boris Petrov, you know."

"Politics is a rich man's game."

"Can they be stopped? Or better, stalled?"

"I knew you were going to ask that. It's your favorite tactic."

"So?"

"For how long?"

"How long do I want them stalled?"

"Yes."

"Maybe a month."

"On what grounds?"

"You know what grounds. I'm in the middle of an investigation."

"Can you be more specific?"

"No."

"Could you be more specific if we weren't yapping on the state's phone lines?"

"Lawyer-client privilege?"

"Of course."

"Tonight?"

"My turf," she said.

"Okay."

"Eight?"

"Perfecto."

THIRTY-FOUR

She didn't turn up until eight-thirty. I had been dozing in my Wrangler when she tapped forcefully on my window. I got out and stared at her. "You were at a meeting looking like that?"

"What's wrong with it?"

"Yoga pants?"

"Everyone wears yoga pants these days."

"That tight?"

"You're not going to go all prudish on me, are you Buddy? I remember a time when I wore tight pants and you couldn't formulate words because you were so interested."

"Point made. Was it your plan for us to converse in front of my car or was going inside a possibility?"

"I knew there was a reason I love you as much as I do."

She escorted me into her building. Her apartment was on the top floor of a ten-story complex in the Silver Lake area of Los Angeles, not terribly far from her downtown offices.

It was a three-bedroom, three-bath luxury dwelling, offering wraparound views that included one of Dodger Stadium. It was designed minimally with little by way of furniture, all of it utilitarian and spare. We sat at a blue Formica table in her kitchen, each of us nursing a snifter of Courvoisier.

She had on an eggshell-blue tunic that hung loosely above her navy yoga pants. Her shoulder-length blond hair fell haphazardly over one eye and she frequently pushed it aside. She emitted a hint of patchouli which, I suddenly remembered, never failed to turn me on. "Were you planning to listen to me or is it your intention to just sit there with that foolish grin plastered on your face?"

"You didn't forget, did you?"

"You mean forget how to ring your chimes?"

"That's right."

"No."

We sat quietly.

"Would you prefer we skip the conversation and make tracks for the bedroom?"

"No. Not at all. You were saying?"

"Could you please explain all that's going on in Buddy World just now?"

"With regards to?"

"Don't be a bore, Buddy. Why is everyone suddenly so interested in you?"

"Boris Petrov is seeking revenge."

"For?"

"Payback for my aggressive behavior regarding the beach access issue. And, more importantly, for not accepting his bribe."

"Why am I guessing there's more?"

"There's every chance he's operating a narcotics laboratory on his property and overseeing its distribution."

"And you know this how?"

"One of his many private soldiers snitched him out."

One who's under an ICE watch?"

"In the the L.A. Metropolitan Detention Center."

"I assume your father knows about this."

"He does."

"And your game plan?"

"I'm going to roust the son of a bitch."

"How?"

"Every couple of weeks an armada of speedboats turns up at the Petrov mansion dock. Usually late at night. That's when he transfers the drugs from his lab to the boats, which then distributes them to wherever they're going. According to my source, Petrov personally supervises the operation."

"And you're going to surprise them."

"That's the plan."

"And if you're right?"

"Mr. Petrov will have a great deal to answer for."

"And if you fail?"

"Failure isn't an option."

"When are you planning to do this?"

"I'm not sure."

"Because?"

"There's no telling when the drop will actually take place. I need enough time to stake it out and be ready to strike when the boats arrive."

"Should I know more?"

"Only that it will be a two-headed strike. Once the troops are engaged in the transfer of the narcotics from the mansion to the dock, that's when we'll hit them at both sites."

"The dock and the mansion?"

"Yes."

"Warrant?"

"I'll have one."

She sat silently for a while. "What about the killings?"

"A mystery."

"That you'll solve how?"

"By the seat of my pants."

"Try not to be so obtuse, Buddy. I'm your lawyer and I'm currently hearing from some of the state's heaviest hitters that you're not fit for the job. And neither is your father, also."

"I'm trying to low-key this thing, Jordy. The killer is way out in front of me. He's meticulous in his planning and his execution. I believe he's killed before. At first we were uncertain it was anything other than a random event but we now have an M.O., which I'm researching nationally in an attempt to match it up with other unsolved killings."

"So you aren't stymied by it?"

"Not in the least. Years of working L.A. Homicide hips you to pretty much everything."

"You know a thing or two because you've seen a thing or two."

"Something like that."

She finished her cognac and poured herself a couple of fingers more. I still had most of mine left.

"Okay," she said.

"Okay what?"

"I can handle this. I'll fend off the Petrov enthusiasts and I'll quietly discuss the killings with the appropriate parties."

"And Petrov's bid for diplomatic status?"

"Trickier."

"So?"

"I'll need to get back to you on it. Timing will play a key role."

"Meaning?"

"How soon will you be mounting your offensive?"

"As soon as possible."

"How about sooner? Without knowing all of the protocols, I can only advise that sooner is better."

"Advice taken." I smiled at her. "Where did we go wrong?"

"I presume you've changed the subject."

"Correct."

"We each wanted the same thing," she said.

"Which was?"

"Independence. Solitude. Freedom. Oh, and did I mention freedom?"

"That's what we wanted?"

"We sure didn't want marriage. Or children. We crossed that

bridge, saw what was on the other side, then whirled around and raced back."

"We did, didn't we?"

"I came closer with you than I'd ever been with anyone, Buddy."

"And?"

"It scared the shit out of me."

"Not only you."

"But we did have a few laughs in the process."

"Along with a handful of orgasms."

"A whole lot more than a handful."

"Sad, really."

"What sad?"

"That we came so close."

"Not sad at all," she said with a sigh. "And if you think so, you're lying to yourself. We both got exactly what we wanted."

"So, what about now?"

"Now?"

"Yes. Now."

"You mean should we rip our clothes off and jump on each other's bones?"

"Something along those lines, yes."

"I don't think so. And neither do you, by the way."

"You think?"

"I know. We've been there, done that. There's nothing to be gained but anxiety and distress."

We were silent for a while.

Then a sly grin lit her face. "At least we'll always have Paris."

THIRTY-FIVE

Something my father told me stuck in my craw. In defining my role in the Petrov affair, he'd dropped the bombshell, "You're a wild card. It's your deal. You own it."

It hadn't quite occurred to me in that manner. Not that I mind owning it; it's that it appears I came to own it without having had any say in the matter.

This whole coastal issue, public access versus private ownership, had been in my consciousness since I was a boy. A teenaged boy who experienced the issue firsthand.

My boyhood pal, Petey Brigham, had moved with his family from Freedom to Point Dume, an exclusive enclave of elegant, costly single-family houses located on a promontory overlooking the Pacific on the Malibu coast.

I had been invited to spend a weekend with the Brighams. Once unpacked and ensconced, Petey and I embarked on an exploratory adventure. We skittered down the promontory to the parking area below and set off for Paradise Cove, arguably the finest beach in the area.

We were ninth-graders, fourteen, our hormones raging, our bodies filling out. Both of us were athletes, a pair of gym rats and body-builders, each destined to make at least two varsities once we entered our respective high schools.

Paradise Cove featured a pristine stretch of sand that was shielded by a wooden pier to the south and a windswept break-water to the north. Its centerpiece was a popular beachfront café just steps away from the surf.

There had been conflicts regarding beach access and parking by those other than café clientele, which caused a number of demonstrations wherein protesters railed that access was as much their right as it was the café's.

Despite Coastal Commission rulings in favor of the protesters, the café owners demurred. They hired attendants who were little more than hooligans, whose job it was to deny access to the parking area by anyone other than café customers. And even more problematic, the job appeared to include denying non-café customers access to the beach as well.

It was an unseasonably warm spring day when Petey Brigham and I sauntered into Paradise Cove. Our intention was to plop ourselves down on the beach and catch some serious rays. A swim or two was also in our plan.

We slipped into the parking lot and lagged behind a quartet of adults who were headed for the café. As we neared the beach, we kicked off our shoes and walked barefoot onto the sand.

I felt the hand grab the back of my shirt before I realized the assailant was one of the parking attendants, a burly young man in his late teens, mean-looking and angry.

"Fuck you think you're going?" he spit out as he whirled me around.

I shook myself free. "What business is it of yours?"

"This here is private property. Scram."

I made eye contact with Petey Brigham, then turned away from the attendant and headed for the shore.

This time the goon tripped me and I fell heavily to the sand. "I guess you don't hear so good," he bellowed. "I said fuck off. You're not welcome here."

"I have as much right as anyone to be here."

"Says you."

"Says me, is right. It's the law. You could look it up."

"You think?" He took a step in my direction. "I already looked it up. Scram."

Holding my hands up preventively, I said, "You'll be making a big mistake if you start anything cute."

"I'm shaking in my boots."

He moved more insistently toward me, which is when I grabbed a handful of sand and flung it directly into his eyes. He grabbed his face as if he'd been shot. I kneed him hard in the nuts. He dropped like a stone.

"Come on, Buddy," Petey said. "Let's get outta here. This isn't going to end well."

We both took off running but not before I threw another handful of sand at the downed thug.

We had caught the attention of the head parking attendant who started screaming to another member of his staff. "Don't let those guys get away. I'm calling the cops."

We shot past the attendant's post and headed away from Paradise Cove, followed at a distance by the other staff member. Once on the coast road, we turned north, in the direction of Point Dume.

Sirens could be heard coming from the south. The staff guy still followed us. I quit running and turned to him. He stopped dead in his tracks.

"Unless you want the same thing your friend got, I'd advise you to quit following us."

Despite the difference in our ages, the boy clearly feared me, daunted by my crazy behavior. He fled. Petey and I made it safely to the Point Dume trail and vanished.

It was then that I came to understand that the interests of private business superseded the rights of the public. Despite the so-called dictates of the Coastal Commission.

What I had yet to learn about was chicanery and bribery.

But in due course I would.

THIRTY-SIX

I had chosen five members for my team: Al Striar, P.J. Lincoln, Dave Balding, and Buzz Farmer. Marsha Russo would be in charge of the command post.

A meeting was scheduled for us to discuss our game plan in detail. I wanted to be fully operational in a matter of days. I summoned Marsha to go over the logistics and determine the materials we would require.

I was seated at the small conference table in the corner of my office when she shuffled in, closed the door behind her, dropped a stack of files on the table, and sat across from me.

"This is about the raid on the Petrov mansion?" she asked.

"I wouldn't exactly call it a raid."

"What would you call it?"

"An operation."

"A raid by any other name."

"Whatever."

"Have you time for another subject before we start?"

"Is it relevant?"

"Of course it's relevant. Why else would I bring it up?"

I nodded.

"You're not going to like it."

"Okay."

"It involves Buzz Farmer."

"Go on."

She resettled herself in her chair and planted her elbows on the table. "You know I've been researching unsolved serial killings."

"I do."

"There are a number of places where cases are still open, some more recent than others. It's the recents that caught my eye. Hartford, Connecticut. St. Louis, Missouri. Atlanta, Georgia. Chicago, Illinois. It was Chicago that got my attention."

"Because?"

"As you taught me, Buddy, I trusted my instincts. I made a cold call to Chicago Police headquarters and reached Captain Art Schimmel, commander of the violent crimes section, Central Division.

"He seemed nice enough, although clearly overwhelmed by the sheer magnitude of his job. He termed it *Dozens of unsolveds. Murder rates through the roof.*"

She stared at me for several moments, deep in thought, uncertain how best to proceed. "He knows Buzz Farmer. Brought his name up without my having to ask. Wondered how Buzz was doing here in Freedom. How he was dealing with the separation."

"Separation?"

"Apparently his wife left him. Took the kids and returned to Rockford."

"Rockford, Illinois?"

"That's where she's from."

"When?"

"You ready?"

"Go on."

"About six weeks after they moved here."

"What?"

"Approximately three months ago."

"How could we not have known?"

"Good question. There's another fact I haven't yet grappled

with."

"That being?"

"If what the commander said is true, she left him nearly coincident with the first killing."

She stared at me, then looked away.

"What aren't you telling me, Marsha?"

"There are a string of unsolved serial killings in Chicago central."

"And that's relevant because?"

"One of the primary detectives was Buzz Farmer."

"So?"

"The killings stopped after he left."

"You're not suggesting he's the killer, are you?"

"Not at all. I know it's not unusual for time gaps to occur between serial killings. I'm just noting an odd coincidence is all."

"But you have suspicions."

"Wouldn't you?"

"I don't really know."

"I'd like to interview the wife. Kelly."

"You mean phone her out of the blue?"

"I mean I want to go there."

"To Rockford?"

"Yes."

"Why?"

"Something's not kosher. If I can look in her eye, woman to woman, maybe I can learn what it is. I don't like this, Buddy."

"You don't like it enough to drag yourself all the way to Chicago?"

"What is it you call it, coply intuition?"

I sat quietly for a while, mulling over her request. "He can't know."

"I understand. Nobody but us can know."

"Okay."

"I wish I felt better about this."

"Me, too."

THIRTY-SEVEN

We set up shop at a family-run motel in the northernmost coastal corner of Santa Barbara County, just south of the San Remo County line. The Friendly Inn was located less than three miles from the Petrov mansion.

The command post was now headed by Wilma Hansen, filling in for Marsha as our logistics coordinator. A longtime veteran of the Sheriff's Department and its current dispatcher, Wilma was a raven-haired dynamo whose caustic wit and infectious laughter provided a welcome relief from the omnipresent stress level of police work. A handsome mother of three, married to a man who owned a highly regarded mechanic's garage. Wilma was a town fixture and a great asset to the department.

Dave Balding was in charge of our transpo contingent, which included a number of different make and model cars and trucks so that members of our team could roam the mansion's exterior without calling attention to themselves by appearing frequently in the same conveyance.

The first order of business was for our resident photographer, P.J. Lincoln, to surreptitiously set up spy cameras in key locations so we could monitor the activity around the mansion and the boat dock.

The plan was for him to enter the grounds as if he were a

tourist. Access to the beach was now unhindered. He was to arrive in the late afternoon, as if he were there to watch the sunset.

The Petrov security detail had been seriously diminished by the removal of so many illegals. A Los Angeles-based security firm had been engaged to replace them. They provided enough personnel to monitor the comings and goings of the visitors to Petrov's beach. But they were far less motivated than the Russians had been, and likely to pay less attention to the exact whereabouts of beachcombers who might wander off.

On day one, after slipping through the mansion's main gate along with a pair of other visitors, P.J. Lincoln meandered away from the approved pathway and ambled through the abundant forest-like grounds, invisible in the late afternoon shadows, making his way to the points we had previously identified as those of prime interest.

In his backpack were a number of tiny battery-operated security cameras that he secreted on various tree branches and verdant shrubbery limbs, each providing unimpeded views of the mansion and the boat dock.

Back at The Friendly Inn, Wilma Hansen and Al Striar peopled a virtual video village where each of P.J.'s cameras fed a corresponding monitor.

Once that was done, we were ready.

THIRTY-EIGHT

Nothing much happened until the night of day three. Buzz Farmer had drawn the video village midnight to six a.m. shift and my cell phone jangled me awake at around four.

"There's activity at the mansion," he said.

"What's going on?"

"A Range Rover arrived a few minutes ago. A short man emerged, mature, well dressed, and imperious-looking. Has to be Petrov. He stretched, took a few deep breaths, and stood looking around for several moments. Then he entered the mansion."

"Let me know if he reappears. Or if anything changes."

"Copy that."

Having been startled awake, I realized getting back to sleep wasn't in the cards.

My thoughts turned to Buzz Farmer. Marsha Russo had bundled herself off to Rockford, Illinois, to interview his wife.

As for Buzz himself, he continued to tirelessly and professionally assist with the Petrov surveillance. But Marsha's revelation disturbed me.

I tried to reconcile the fervent appeals he made on behalf of his candidacy for the job with the knowledge that his wife had left him. Three months ago.

I now had misgivings regarding Mr. Farmer. Nothing specific.

Nothing I could put my finger on. But I found his dispassionate nature odd. He made all the right moves and said all the right things, but he did and said them mechanically.

I was hoping that Marsha's interview would prove benign and that his behavior was nothing more than idiosyncratic.

But he bothered me. More so than I wanted to admit.

• • ● • •

I readied myself for the day, then headed to The Friendly Inn dining room where I joined Wilma Hanson for an early breakfast.

We reviewed our plans for the deployment of each member of the team. Positions would be manned at dusk, after Petrov's rented security forces had departed for the day. Back and shoulder packs were to be checked and rechecked to make certain the correct weapons wound up in the right hands.

We established three main staging areas inside the compound.

The first was at the outer edge of a heavily forested foothill that opened onto a section of beach that fronted the dock and the boathouse.

The second was amid the Japanese privet hedges and the tall Northwind and Prairie Sky switch grasses that combined to surround the mansion's immaculately manicured front lawn with its three-hole putting green, fishpond, and redwood gazebo.

The third area was halfway between the first two, in a brambled glen bordering the inland side of the sandy roadway that ran between the house and the dock.

A member of our team was to be stationed at each of these locations.

Anticipating we'd conduct an action that very night, we arranged for a previously organized team of ten San Remo County Police officers to assemble at twilight in The Friendly Inn parking lot, where they would stand ready to assist, should it prove necessary.

We recruited these officers because of their experience under fire. All of them had seen combat in places such as Kabul and Baghdad.

The day crept by slowly, unimpeded by any unusual activity at either the dock or the mansion. Boris Petrov remained secluded inside.

At six o'clock, the hired security guards rounded up any remaining beachgoers, escorted them from the grounds, then closed and locked the access gates. Satisfied all was in order, the guards left the area in a gray Honda SUV.

Shortly after eight p.m., with darkness swiftly descending, Al Striar arrived at the estate's southernmost access point brandishing a heavy-duty wire cutter that he used to snip open a flap in the fencing.

One by one, each member of the team wriggled through and swiftly headed to his appointed station. By the time darkness had fully fallen, we were all at our posts, ready for whatever the night might bring.

Buzz and I were hidden together in the brambles, not noted for comfort but well shielded. He seemed withdrawn, distant, absent.

"You okay?"

He looked at me as if for the first time. "What? Oh, sorry. This operation puts me in mind of the Afghani nights. The nights of terror. All of us preparing strategically for a firefight and at the same time, trying to ward off our collective fear of sudden death. God, it was horrible. I'm sorry, Buddy. I'll be okay."

"You sure?"

"Yeah. Not to worry."

Shortly after eight-thirty, Boris Petrov sprang from the mansion accompanied by two men dressed in white lab coats, each sporting a pair of black canvas shoulder bags. They moved swiftly along the sandy road that led to the dock.

At about the same time, we could hear the roar of boat engines coming from the sea.

"It's on," I texted Wilma. She, in turn, transmitted the information to the team.

Buzz Farmer and I were hidden amid the tall switch grasses, watching Petrov and his associates make their way up the road.

Despite his height, Petrov walked with a loping gait and a swagger that accentuated how lithe and graceful he was. He wore a collared gray sweatshirt over tailored blue jeans. He had on gray Nike high-tops. He exhibited an air of invincibility and power, someone to be reckoned with.

I tore my attention away from him and turned to Buzz. "You ready?"

"Beyond ready."

"Shall we?"

"My pleasure."

Buzz made a furtive dash for the mansion where he would connect with Johnny Kennerly and P.J. Lincoln.

I set out for the dock, ducking in and out of the shadows, careful not to reveal myself to Petrov and the two Lab Coats in front of me. I arrived moments after Al Striar and Dave Balding.

Under the cover of darkness, we were close enough to watch Petrov and the Lab Coats greeting two other men at the dock, men to whom they handed over the four canvas shoulder bags.

After handshakes all around, and nodding to Boris Petrov, the Lab Coats left the dock and headed back to the mansion.

As the sound of the boat engines neared, one of the dockhands flipped the switch on the boathouse power panel which activated a pair of high voltage lighting fixtures that rested on fifteen-foot-high towers.

That was our cue.

Striar and Balding, their weapons drawn, made tracks for the two men on the dock, each of whom, their eyes still adjusting to the intense light, finally spotted the approaching deputies and immediately reached for their weapons.

"Police officers," Striar shouted. "Hands in the air."

This caught Boris Petrov's attention, distracting him enough to allow me to furtively creep up behind him. I startled him when I thrust my Colt Commander into the small of his back.

He suddenly whirled and lashed out at me, kicking and pummeling me repeatedly with his fists. I backed into a defensive position, feinted left, caught sight of an opening, and unloaded a hard right jab into the side of his head, followed by a fast left cross and a right uppercut that dropped him.

As he lay inert on the sandy road, groaning, I removed a plastic tie from my kit belt and secured his hands behind him.

Still groggy, he struggled slowly to his feet and glared at me through steely blue eyes, rife with venom. "You," he sneered.

"We meet again."

"A meeting you'll soon come to regret."

"Regrets are a two-way street, Boris. As you'll soon come to realize."

He glared at me.

"Did I forget to mention you're under arrest?"

"Arrest?"

"Yes."

"For what reason?"

"Too many to go into just now."

"You're an insignificant man, Mr. Buddy. You have no idea who or what you're dealing with."

"Yikes. Now you've given me the shivers."

The sound of men yelling caught my attention. I looked up in time to see Al Striar head-butt one of Petrov's men, knocking him off balance. He then jumped on the man, grabbed him by the ears, and slammed his head heavily into the ground.

Dave Balding was also on the move, racing toward the dock where the second man had already picked up two of the four canvas bags and hurled them into the sea.

Balding, his Sig Sauer service revolver in hand, called out to him as he reached for the other two bags. "Stop right there."

Undaunted, the man unholstered a Glock G43 semi and turned it on Balding.

Dave shot first, but it went wide.

In turn, the man fired at Dave, hitting him in the leg, knocking him off of his feet.

My Colt was already in hand, and when the man stepped over to the fallen Balding with the intention of finishing him, I shot the gun from his hand.

He gaped at me in amazement, then grabbed his hand which now had three fewer fingers than it did when the shooting started. And it had begun to bleed profusely.

The speedboats were just rounding the jetty when the shots rang out. Leaving a churning wake behind them, the boats hastily reversed course and headed back out to sea.

In the chaos of the gunfire, Boris Petrov had slipped away. I spotted him running full bore toward the mansion.

Leaving Striar to deal with the downed men, the two remaining shoulder bags, and the wounded Dave Balding, I took off after Petrov.

He was in good physical condition and despite his height, ran faster than I might have imagined. Even with his hands bound behind him. In a final burst of speed, he outraced me to the mansion, hot-footed it up the front steps, and disappeared inside.

I clambered up the steps after him, but when I entered the house, there was no sign of him.

I found myself standing in a huge antechamber, all marble and dark woods. Shafts of diffused light insinuated themselves through floor-to-ceiling stained-glass windows. A massive mahogany staircase climbed skyward toward a balcony-surrounded second-floor landing.

I noticed an ancient Otis elevator cage containing a gold and steel filigree cab carved into one of the walls, an option for those not hardy enough to attempt the stairs.

As I stood somewhat dumbfounded, Johnny Kennerly showed up in the foyer.

"Buddy," he exclaimed. "What are you doing here?"

"Looking for Boris Petrov. He beat me by only seconds."

"I haven't seen him."

"He came barreling in here. He's got to be around some-where."

"I wouldn't know. P.J. and I have been searching for the lab, but we haven't found it."

"How difficult could it be to find?"

"Good question."

Buzz Farmer appeared at the top of the staircase and called down to us. "What's up?"

"Have you seen Petrov?"

"No. Should I have?"

"He came plowing into the house and then vanished."

"Well, he's not upstairs. I would have seen him."

"He has to be somewhere. He didn't just dematerialize."

"This is a weird place," Johnny said. "P.J. and I have been all over it and haven't found even a trace of any pharmaceutical laboratory."

"You think there are hidden rooms?"

"Wouldn't surprise me," Johnny said.

"So Petrov could have slipped into one of them. Even the lab rooms might be hidden."

"It's possible."

"How can we find out?"

"Anyone have a fire axe?" Buzz asked as he made his way downstairs.

Johnny Kennerly spoke up. "Listen, Buddy, for all we know, he could be climbing out of a manhole in downtown Freedom right now. Like El Chapo."

THIRTY-NINE

It wasn't long before the lawyers arrived.

Dave Balding had been bundled off to a nearby hospital. As was the man whose hand I shot. The captive Petrov employee was en route to a Freedom township jail cell.

Al Striar had retrieved two of the four canvas shoulder bags, each carrying enough copycat Fentanyl tablets to provide opiate fixes for half the population of San Francisco. But, try as we might, we couldn't solve the mystery of the disappearing oligarch.

Two attorneys from the Hobart Law Firm, local associates of Leonard, Howard and Arthur, emerged from a black Lexus sedan and red-faced, demanded we leave the property.

"Immediately," emphasized Judy May, the duo's spokesperson.

"Not going to happen," I said coldly.

"I beg your pardon?"

"A crime has been committed on this property and we have no plans to leave here until our investigation has been completed."

"You'll force me to call the police."

"We are the police."

"The District Attorney, then."

"Look, Ms. May, we have no intention of vacating these premises until we locate Mr. Petrov."

"Mr. Petrov is not present at this location."

"I followed him into the house. I know he's here."

"You're wrong."

I stood staring at her silently.

"If you're so sure he's here, why don't you lead me to him?"

"I'm unable to do that."

She turned to her associate. "Make the call, Robert."

Robert nodded, punched several numbers into his cell phone and stepped away to speak privately.

I looked at Johnny Kennerly. "Keep going, John."

He nodded, gathered the troops, and headed back inside.

In short order, District Attorney Michael Lytell's name popped up on my cell phone.

"Buddy Steel," I answered.

"Call it off, Buddy," Lytell ordered.

I, too, wandered away so as to speak privately. "There's ample evidence of a crime having been committed here, Mike. And Petrov was definitely involved in it."

'His lawyers say the opposite. They claim he's not even on the property."

"He is. I apprehended him but in the confusion, he eluded me. He's somewhere inside the mansion, more than likely in some kind of secret enclosure."

"A secret enclosure? Really?"

"Don't minimize this, Mike."

"Can you produce him?"

"Not at the moment."

"Listen to me, Buddy. This Petrov character is a person of some considerable importance to the Russian President. I've already heard directly from the Governor about it. If you can't put your finger on him, you'll have to stand down."

"I could start tearing down walls. I know he's secreted somewhere inside them."

"You want to start destroying the mansion? You think that's going to fly?"

"I've got the appropriate warrant."

"To search, not destroy."

"I know he's here, Mike."

"Knowing and actually proving are two different things."

"I have a pair of suitcases filled with synthetic Fentanyl. I saw him and two of his associates carry these opioids from the mansion to his boat dock with the intention of loading them onto a trio of speedboats."

"Fingerprints?"

"Excuse me?"

"Do these suitcases have his DNA on them?"

"Uncertain. They were carried by his associates."

"Is there any other evidence?"

"Not yet."

"That being the case, I hereby instruct you to close up shop and get out of there, Buddy. Don't belabor this."

After a pause, I said, "This isn't over, Mike. Not by a long shot."

FORTY

Having made certain that at least one of our officers was stationed just outside the mansion's gate, but in full view of each of its two major access points, I headed back to the station.

On top of my message pile was one from Marsha Russo, who was still in Rockford. I returned the call.

"I made contact with the wife, Buddy."

"And?"

"She doesn't want to meet with me."

"Did she say why?"

"Something in the neighborhood of it's none of my business."

"What neighborhood?"

"The '*Fuck off*' neighborhood."

"So, what do you do next?"

"She's living with her parents. I know their address and I'm heading there now."

"With no assurance she'll see you."

"Oh, she'll see me, all right."

"How do you figure that?"

"I'm very persuasive."

"What's your plan?"

"My plan?"

"How do you plan on getting her to see you?"

"The old foot in the door gambit."

"The foot in the door gambit?"

"You have a better idea?"

My next call was to my father, whom I found in his office here at the station. He invited me to join him. "Curiouser and curiouser," he said when I told him about my experience with Boris Petrov.

"He's some piece of business, this Russian of yours."

"So, what do you advise?"

"Hard to say because there's this gathering storm of opposition that wants to smother you."

"You're not suggesting I drop it, are you?"

"Not in this lifetime. I like what you're doing."

"This gathering storm, as you put it, is comprised of a host of self-righteous, self-serving, self-important plutocrats including, I might add, the Russian president."

"Daunting."

"You think?"

"Look, Buddy. You knew you were up against some kind of inexorable force when you set out on this adventure. This Petrov is unlike anyone you, or even I for that matter, have ever come up against. He plays in an entirely different league.

"But you won the first round. And you're close to having enough on him to open a full scale investigation into whatever it is he's doing. The man you shot is in custody. As is his partner. A couple of Petrov's bodyguard contingent are still sitting in a Los Angeles jail awaiting extradition. Use them to help you find the pharmacists in the white lab coats. And when you find them, squeeze the sons of bitches. Get this Russian dickhead dead to rights and then see how the so-called gathering storm plays out. I'm betting it'll be like rats in a sinking ship.

"And use that lawyer of yours as a buffer. She said she could help deflect Petrov's efforts to stop you. Hold her feet to that fire."

He hadn't finished but was still formulating what he wanted to tell me. "And do me a favor," he said finally.

"What?"

"Keep your gun with you at all times. Locked and loaded. Sleep with it under your pillow."

"Because?"

"This guy's lethal. Lethal. Amoral. Unethical. Totally unpredictable. So you'll want to talk softly and carry a big stick."

"Or a high-powered, semi-automatic weapon."

"That, too."

FORTY-ONE

I was back in the reflective garden with Vlad Smirnik, who was none too happy to be there.

The effects of his incarceration coupled with uncertainty had dampened his spirits. He appeared dejected as he collected himself to go another round with me. "You want more information? And you think I'll give it to you because?"

"I'm your only friend."

"With friends like you..."

"Look, Vlad. The more you assist in my investigation, the more receptive the judge will be regarding your petition."

"My petition?"

"You want to stay in the United States, right?"

"Right."

"And I've pledged to help you win that battle, right?"

"Right."

"So why would you choose to defy me?"

"Because you agreed to help me based on the information I gave you earlier. Now you want more. What's to stop you from seeking even more?"

"Nothing."

"Excuse me?"

"There's nothing to stop me."

"So you admit it."

"Listen to me, Vlad. I'm on your side. One of the secondary reasons I came here today was to get your grandmother's and your mother's names. I have a proposal for the District Attorney."

"What proposal?"

"Answer my questions and I'll tell you."

Smirnik stood and stared blank-eyed at the garden. He spotted a dead branch on one of the English ivy bushes and broke it off. He started to pace. Then suddenly he stopped. "Ask."

"Hidden rooms?"

"What about them?"

"Can you confirm their existence?"

"Yes."

"A passageway?"

"What about it?"

"Where is it?"

"I don't know."

"Why don't you know?"

"I only heard about it. I was rarely, if ever, inside the house. I was perimeter security. An outdoor guy."

"How did you hear about it?"

"One of the Russians. A bodyguard. With a big mouth."

"And he told you about hidden rooms?"

"He said his pharmacist friend told him about them."

"His pharmacist friend?"

"Yes."

"Did he tell you this friend's name?"

Smirnik didn't answer. He looked away.

"Did he tell you his name?"

"No."

"Wrong answer, Vlad."

"Look, I don't really know any of the pharmacists. They kept to themselves. Very exclusive. Separate from the rest of us."

"But your friend knew one of them. How so?"

"The guy had relatives in St. Petersburg."

"What's the guy's name?"

Smirnik began fidgeting. "If I tell you, they'll know it was me."

"And you fear retribution."

"They'll know it was me."

"You're in no danger, Vlad."

"You don't know these guys."

"Most of them are gone. Only a small handful are still in detention awaiting deportation. You're not in any danger."

"My friend mentioned only a single name. When he was tooting his own horn about how important he was."

"What's the name?"

"Yashin."

"First or last?"

"Last."

"A pharmacist named Yashin."

"Yes."

He stared at me hard-eyed. "Now it's your turn," he said. "Tell me your idea."

"If I'm right, you may be an American citizen."

"How do you figure?"

"You said your mother was born in Russia, yes?"

"Yes."

"The child of an American citizen."

"I guess that's right. My grandmother was born in Cleveland."

"And raised there?"

"Yes."

"And she renounced her citizenship, but some time after your mother was born. Yes?"

"That's what she said."

"If it's true, you're entitled to claim your American citizenship."

"No shit."

"And I know just the lawyer to argue your case."

"Who?"

"After I confirm what you told me."

"So I still have to wait."

"Yes."

"And you could just as easily want even more than I've already given you."

"Correct."

"So, am I a schmuck or what?"

"I'm angling for the '*or what*.'"

FORTY-TWO

Sleeplessness was my curse, and just a matter of minutes after finally entering dreamland, my cell phone started ringing.

I took a quick glance at my watch and found that it was seven o'clock and that I'd been asleep for nearly three hours.

"It's Buddy," I said.

"We've got another one," Wilma Hansen announced.

"Another one what?"

"Just like the other three. Dead in the car. This time it's a man."

"Where?"

She told me.

"Who's there?"

"Kennerly and Lincoln."

"Buzz Farmer?"

"Day off."

"I'm on my way."

"You're sure you're awake enough to drive?"

"Yes."

"How can you tell?"

Once again we were downtown, this time in a low-rent neighborhood. Strip malls interspersed with two- and three-story apartment buildings. Street parking was ample, and undeveloped lots served as repositories for all sorts of debris, including automobile parts and tire remnants.

As in the earlier killings, a late model Volvo had been attacked as it pulled away from a metered parking space, its front end sticking out into the road. The driver's side window had been shattered and, once again, we were looking at an unholy mess of shattered glass and bloody matter.

No visible clues presented themselves. No spy cameras were in the vicinity.

"Another zero burger," Johnny Kennerly said as we examined the scene.

"And the victim's family will express astonishment as to why this event occurred."

"What do you want to do, Buddy?"

"You mean aside from making it all go away?"

He gave me his *not funny* look.

"Run all of the forensic drills. Who knows? Maybe we'll get lucky."

"And maybe buffaloes will fly, too."

When I finally arrived at the office, having wended my way through a burgeoning crowd of shouting reporters, there was a message from Marsha Russo. I was a bit surprised she hadn't called my cell phone, but when I checked my phone holster, I realized I had left it at home. Remembering to carry it is one of life's great challenges. Once a Luddite, always one.

I caught her at O'Hare Airport, preparing to board her return flight to L.A. "You heard," I asked.

"About the killing?"

"Yes."

"Wilma told me."

"Did you see her?"

"Of course I saw her. I'm Wonder Woman, remember?"

"What did you learn?"

"He had been behaving strangely."

"Meaning?"

"They had been high school sweethearts and soon after his graduation from the University of Illinois Police Training Institute, they married.

"Following a year spent as a consultant to Hamid Karzai's personal security force in Kabul, Afghanistan, he returned home and joined the Rockford Police Department.

"She interpreted his noticeable stress level as a sign, not only of post-warfare anguish, but also of his anxiety over having to readjust to life in America and at the same time, make both a living and a name for himself.

"Apparently the stress worsened when they relocated to Chicago, a move they made in the hope of building a better life in a larger pond. She attributed the distance that was growing between them to the strain of starting a new job in a strange city where the level of violence was redolent of what he experienced in Afghanistan. She claims she made every effort to help ease the pressure, but he became even more withdrawn.

"After their first child was born, she said Buzz became obsessed with an imagined image of him being shot in the line of duty and leaving the baby fatherless."

"Nothing too far out of the ordinary for a young cop," I interjected.

"They quickly had a second child and that rattled him even further. That was when he began searching for police work elsewhere. By the time they arrived here, she felt completely cut off from him emotionally. Her words.

"Instead of welcoming the change from big city to small-town life and the reduction of his stress level, he worsened. She said he was rarely home and when he was, he was moody and uncommunicative."

"Doesn't sound like the Buzz Farmer we know."

"If, indeed, we know him."

"And she left him because of that?"

"She left him because he throttled her."

"He choked her?"

"Once."

"And?"

"Once was enough for her. She'd had her fill of him. Her parents came out from Rockford and when he was at work, they packed her stuff, gathered the kids and the dog, and returned home to Illinois."

"And he never told anyone?"

"He certainly didn't tell us."

"And this was how long ago?"

"Three months."

"Around the time the killings began."

"But not necessarily connected to them."

"True."

Neither of us spoke for several moments.

"Anyway, I'm on my way back."

"Okay."

"Did you miss me?"

"I can't remember."

"You can't remember whether or not you missed me?"

"Yes."

"You know something, Buddy?"

"What?"

"You're a total dickhead."

"Thank you."

No sooner had the call ended when Buzz Farmer appeared in my doorway. "You busy?"

I looked up at him. He was unshaven and out of uniform. I motioned for him to come in. He sat opposite me.

"I'm sorry I wasn't there," he began. "I just heard it on the news."

"It's your day off."

"It is. But I want to help. Is there anything I can do?"

"I don't think so, Buzz. Johnny and Al are on the scene, which is not a whole lot different from the other three."

"The location?"

"Not in Freedom center. Close, though. Working-class neighborhood. Mostly apartment buildings and small businesses."

"Car sticking into the middle of the road?"

"Yes."

"I'm available if you need me, Buddy."

"Enjoy your day off, Buzz. Spend it with your family. I'm sure they'll appreciate it."

"They would if they were here."

"They're not here?"

"They're in Illinois. Visiting Kelly's parents."

"I didn't know."

"It's okay. I'll survive."

"I should hope so. But I still have nothing for you to do. Go home. Get some rest. It's been a long week."

"You sure?"

"I'm sure."

"Okay. Thanks, Buddy." He headed for the door.

"When are they due back?"

"Excuse me?"

"Kelly and the kids. When are they coming back?"

"Sometime next week."

"And you're okay with them gone?"

"Yeah. Pizza and Chinese takeout. Lots of TV."

"Well, don't get into any trouble."

"I never get into trouble."

"Lucky you."

FORTY-THREE

The conference call had been set for three o'clock, and at the appointed time, the operator took the role.

"Mr. Lytell," she asked.

"Here."

The same procedure followed with Skip Wilder, Jordyn Yates, Sheriff Burton Steel, Sr., and me.

After giving us a number to call should we encounter any difficulties, the operator vanished.

Without any preliminaries, District Attorney Lytell kicked off the proceedings. "You've been sued, Buddy."

"By whom?" Jordyn Yates asked.

"By the firm Leonard, Howard and Arthur, on behalf of the Shoreline Sanctuary Corporation."

"I'm presuming that's a Boris Petrov shell company," Jordyn commented.

"Likely," Lytell said.

"The charges?" Jordyn asked.

"You name it. Illegal search and seizure. Harassment. Defamation of character. Aggravated assault. And get this...disturbing the peace."

"That's all a load of crap and you know it," Jordyn said. "The Sheriff's Department has photographic evidence that Boris Petrov was present at the scene of a crime that had been engineered by him and perpetrated by his employees, two of whom are in custody. We have evidence that proves he was manufacturing and distributing illegal narcotics. He resisted arrest. The Sheriff's Department has him dead to rights."

"That's not what Team Petrov is claiming."

"They're lying."

"The State Department has made inquiries on Petrov's behalf."

"Such as?"

"They want hard evidence. Mr. Petrov is in the process of being vetted for a diplomatic position at the request of the Russian government. The Secretary of State has appealed to the Governor, requesting he intervene.

"The Governor, in turn, petitioned me as to why the Sheriff is hassling a prominent Russian diplomat instead of investing himself in solving a series of violent killings that continue to occur in his county. And that's not all. He wants to know if the duly elected Sheriff is even participating in the investigation. He's claiming the Sheriff is incapable of fulfilling the responsibilities he was elected to perform."

"Sheriff Steel?" Jordyn asked.

"Here," Burton said.

"Can you inform the District Attorney as to your current whereabouts?"

"I'm in my office."

"At the courthouse?"

"That's where it's located."

"And are you performing your duties as you understand them?"

"I am."

"That's a load of crap, Burton," DA Lytell chimed in. "You know damn good and well that Buddy's doing your job while you're experiencing health issues."

"It's true that Buddy is working beside me, but my health is improving and I'm in my office regularly. As for the serial killings, we are pursuing the investigation with vigor."

When Lytell didn't say anything, the Sheriff continued. "And for your information, Mike, we're making significant progress."

"What kind of progress."

"Can I swear you to secrecy?"

I could hear Lytell cover the mouthpiece of the receiver with his hand and bellow to Skip Wilder, "Again with the secrecy."

Wilder replied, "Do it."

Lytell emitted a heavy sigh. "Okay. Secrecy it is."

"We have a person of interest," Burton said.

"Who?"

"You'll know when it's time for you to know."

Again the mouthpiece was covered. "He's got nothing."

"Might I interject a comment?" I said.

"Ah, the prodigal son speaks."

"In answer to your questions, please note that our department is interviewing a number of witnesses to Boris Petrov's participation in significant criminal activity. And as for the serial killings, our investigation has turned promising."

Before Lytell could speak, Jordyn Yates did. "On behalf of my client, I want you to know that we will challenge any and all allegations made by Petrov's shell company.

"We will also call attention to the bullying tactics employed by the Leonard, Howard and Arthur law firm and their heinous misuse of the legal system in an attempt to interfere with an ongoing criminal investigation.

"Sheriff Steel and Deputy Sheriff Steel are deeply invested in bringing all of the guilty parties to justice. And that includes this as yet unauthorized diplomat, Boris Petrov.

"Perhaps you might inform the Governor it's in his best interests to defend the rights of the American people, as opposed to those of a Russian drug lord. This call is over," she said and ended it.

FORTY-FOUR

I was sitting on the overstuffed armchair in my living room, in front of the picture window at twilight, watching the flickering lights of the homes on the Freedom hillside, when the phone rang.

I answered it reluctantly.

"Please hold for Her Honor Mayor Goodnow," a voice dripping with officiousness responded.

She came on almost immediately. "I'm being inundated here, Buddy. What in the hell is going on?"

"And a fine good evening to you, too, Regina."

"Don't fine good evening me. I'm being hounded by media outlets I've never even heard of. I've even been contacted by Sean Hannity's people."

"Wow. Lucky you."

"Don't make jokes, Buddy. People here are scared. They want information. I need to tell them something."

"Tell them the investigation is ongoing."

"They want more than that."

"Look, Regina. We have a serial killer on the loose here. Off the record, we've drawn a bead on a person of interest. But there's not enough evidence yet to make an arrest and bring charges. But again off the record, I'm encouraged."

"Oh, swell. You do realize that this thing is threatening to envelop your father? He, as you well know, is in no position to face any kind of scrutiny. You have to conclude this investigation, Buddy. Or there will be serious consequences."

"What is it you propose I do, Regina?"

"Just what I said. Speed things up. I can't keep these hounds at bay for much longer."

"You're a media queen, Regina. Handle it."

When she said nothing further, I ended the call.

It had gone dark since I first sat down and I was aware of the coastal cloud cover that now allowed only passing glimpses of the three-quarter moon.

Night sounds were insinuating themselves into the early evening din. Crickets. Snatches of windblown musical threads. The occasional helicopter. I could smell wood burning in a nearby fireplace.

Regina's call raised my hackles. I was overrun with disquieting thoughts, many of them regarding Buzz Farmer.

The case tormented me. Although Marsha's news was potentially damning, I still had insufficient proof that it was Buzz.

It also worried me that my father might be dragged into it. He had invested a great deal of optimism in the clinical testing of this as yet unproven chemical. His focus was by and large on the minute-by-minute evolution of his body's response to it. He was constantly on guard for even the slightest change, his mood dependent on his findings.

Although he was present, he was emotionally absent, distracted, and fearful. He was a different person, self-absorbed in an uncharacteristic manner, drum-beating about the vast improvement of his condition, yet all the while emanating abject terror at the prospect of his inexorable decline.

Regina was right. He would be no match for the aggressive media.

This, coupled with the ongoing Petrov mishigas, dampened my spirit.

Let's just say I've had better days.

FORTY-FIVE

The California State Board of Pharmacy confirmed that an Albert Yashin had registered with them following his graduation from the University of the Pacific's Thomas J. Long School of Pharmacy and Health Sciences, located in Stockton, California, class of 2014.

It was when I tried to learn Mr. Yashin's current address that I ran into trouble.

"We're not permitted to give out that information," the voice of an older woman informed me.

After I identified myself, the woman still refused to divulge Yashin's whereabouts.

"May I speak with your supervisor?"

"I have no supervisor."

"Is there someone in the university hierarchy I can speak with?"

"Not about past graduates."

"Tell me your name again, please?"

"I never told you my name."

"Would you tell me now?"

There was silence for a while. Then she said, "Carolyn Daffron."

"Pleased to meet you, Ms. Daffron. As I mentioned, I'm investigating a serious crime and Mr. Yashin is a material witness."

"I can't divulge his address, regardless."

"Is there a reason you're being so intransigent?"

"Rules."

"And you and you alone are the arbiter of these rules?"

"I am."

"And you see fit to deny the County Sheriff information you possess that's valuable to a criminal investigation."

"Rules are rules."

"May I tell you something, Ms. Daffron?"

"Tell me what?"

"You're making a grievous error in judgment."

"That's one opinion."

"So it is. But if you continue to refuse me this information, I will so inform the Sheriff of San Joaquin County of your actions and, in the interests of reciprocity, he will send two deputies to your office at the university and they will arrest you and charge you with obstruction of justice.

"This charge, in turn, will be called to the attention of the office of the President of the university, accompanied by a complaint from the Sheriff's Department regarding your obstructionist behavior.

"Your autonomy, Ms. Daffron, will be seriously jeopardized, as most certainly will your job. The sight of you being frog-marched out of your office in handcuffs won't be pretty. And afterward, everyone watching the evening news will be treated to footage of you being loaded into a Sheriff's van, handcuffed and chained, and bolted to the floor."

A brief silence followed.

"You said you wanted Albert Yashin's current address?" Carolyn Daffron gasped.

"I did say that, yes."

She provided it.

FORTY-SIX

I was parked in front of a four-unit converted town house in a neighborhood filled with them, located at the southernmost edge of San Joaquin County, interspersed amid a number of low-rise apartment buildings, all adhering to height restrictions imposed decades earlier.

An ancient Lincoln Town Car occupied one of the four spaces in front of the weathered town house, which was badly in need of fresh paint. I had asked Marsha Russo to run the license plate and she reported back it was registered to an Albert Yashin.

I exited the Wrangler and meandered around the building, checking the various exit points, winding up at the front door where I found Mr. Yashin's name listed for apartment 2R2.

The front door was locked and, rather than ringing the bell, I returned to the rear of the building and tested the exit door there. When it, too, proved to be locked, I removed a small metal filing device from my pocket, inserted it into the lock and popped the door open.

I stepped into a lobby that was utilitarian, clean and well maintained. A single staircase led to the second floor, where I found apartment 2R2.

I rang the bell and stepped aside, away from the brassbound peephole. Within moments, I noticed its cover sliding away and heard a voice inquire who was there.

"Police," I said and held my badge in front of the peephole.

"What do you want?"

"I'm looking for Albert Yashin."

"Why?"

"Are you Albert Yashin?"

Silence.

"I'm here on police business, Mr. Yashin. Please open the door."

After several more moments, I heard the tumbler turn and saw the door open a crack.

"Proof," Yashin said.

I showed him my badge and ID.

With a sigh he closed the door, undid the chain and then opened it to admit me. I stepped inside.

Albert Yashin was a heavyset, olive-skinned man in his thirties. On his prominent nose rested thick-rimmed glasses through which he stared at me with wide-eyed concern. He had on a light-green hooded sweatshirt and khaki slacks.

"What is it you want?"

"A chat."

"About what?"

"Boris Petrov."

Yashin's restless eyes registered alarm and he instinctively shrank backward. I asked if we might sit, and regaining a measure of composure, he led me into a small living room. Its main point of focus was an oversized, wall-mounted flat-screen TV. A two-seater sofa and a pair of tired armchairs faced it, as did two side tables with matching brass-based lamps.

He pointed me to the sofa. He sat in the adjacent armchair. "What is it you want to know?"

"What exactly you do for Mr. Petrov."

"I occasionally work for him."

"Doing what?"

"This and that."

"By which you mean?"

"Just that. I do the occasional odd job for him."

"I'm not really warming to this conversation, Mr. Yashin. You're a registered pharmacist. What need for your pharmaceutical services would Mr. Petrov have?"

Yashin sat silently.

I leaned forward. "This can go easy or hard. It's up to you. We know that Petrov is a player in the drug trade. We're aware of the full-scale laboratory he has secreted in his home. We know you're an accomplice to the development and manufacture of illegal narcotics.

"You face serious penalties for your crimes, Mr. Yashin, and to that end I've come to make you a one-time offer that will expire within moments of my having made it."

His attention turned inward and after a short stretch of introspection, it returned to me.

"I want you to confirm that your primary function for Mr. Petrov is assisting in the manufacture of opioids. Synthetic Fentanyl, to be exact. I also want you to lead me to the hidden laboratory in which you worked."

"That's all?"

"That and a signed statement."

"And if I don't cooperate?"

"I did mention something about serious consequences, didn't I?"

"And if I cooperate?"

"Try to understand that life as you know it has just taken a serious turn for the worse, Mr. Yashin. You can be cooperative or obstructive. But if I were you, I'd surely opt for cooperation. It might earn you immunity from prosecution. But, hey, it's up to you."

I glanced at my watch. "You have about thirty seconds to decide."

In considerably less than thirty seconds, he said, "Okay. I'll cooperate."

I stood. "Shall we?"

"May I get a few things first?"

"Such as?"

"My phone. My watch."

"No."

"Why no?"

"Because you won't be needing them."

I took his arm and together we headed for the door. Suddenly, he wrested his arm from my grasp. He glared at me.

"I need my house keys."

I smiled. "Why didn't you say so?"

FORTY-SEVEN

It took close to an hour to make the drive from Yashin's house to Freedom. We swung south onto Highway 101 and hugged the shoreline for most of the drive.

Yashin sat silently staring out the window. He appeared to be freighted with the knowledge that his life had indeed changed, and the worry that the change might result in a lengthy incarceration.

I felt his stare. "How do I earn this so-called immunity?"

"You fully cooperate."

"And if I do?"

"You're a small fish in this affair, Mr. Yashin. The government is likely to offer you liberty in exchange for information that leads to the conviction of Boris Petrov."

"I don't know a whole hell of a lot. I'm a minor cog in the wheel and my knowledge of that wheel was restricted to the pharmacology part."

"You were involved in the manufacture of opioids, yes?"

"Yes."

"And you were paid for that."

He nodded.

"How were you paid?"

"In cash."

"Did you receive a tax form?"

"For what I was paid?"

"Yes."

"No."

"Did you file with the IRS?"

"Yes."

"For the full amount?"

He remained silent.

"I'll take that as a no."

"Did you and Petrov ever talk?"

"Once or twice."

"About your work?"

"About the weather. We never discussed work."

"Why?"

"He said the less I knew, the better. He was a very close-mouthed guy."

We pulled into the Sheriff's Department parking lot, where were met by P.J. Lincoln and Marsha Russo.

"What happens now?" Yashin asked.

"You'll be ushered to a cozy accommodation where you'll remain until it's convenient for us to access the Petrov property, and you can lead us to the hidden laboratory."

"How long will that take?"

"As long as it needs to take."

He nodded, his face a portrait of despair.

I asked P.J. to read him his rights. P.J. nodded and led him away.

Once they were gone, I said to Marsha, "Please arrange for a forensics team to scour Yashin's apartment from top to bottom. Confiscate his cell phone and any computers he might have. Print everything of interest on them. This son of a bitch is going down."

"He looks like a little lost lamb."

"A little lost lamb who manufactured enough synthetic Fentanyl to wipe out a major city. We'll be leading this particular lamb to the slaughter."

"But he doesn't know that."

"No."

"And he's going to spring the lock on the hidden door for you."

"So he says."

"For which he thinks he's going to be rewarded with some kind of clemency."

"He does."

"Which you suggested to him."

"Yes. But I lied."

"Is that cricket, Buddy?"

"Cricket? This guy is a reprehensible lowlife. Responsible for untold numbers of deaths. He willingly applied his pharmacological skills to the service of despicability. I'm going to do all I can to make certain he's held accountable.

"Cricket? Talk cricket to the grieving families whose loved ones died as a result of his actions."

FORTY-EIGHT

Marsha was planted in the chair opposite my desk, an overstuffed file on her lap, glasses pushed up on her forehead, reading aloud from handwritten notes she had amassed in a spiral-ringed notebook.

"Here's one I'm sure you'll enjoy," she said. "There are two unsolved murders in the Rockford, Illinois, police files. Both occurred six years ago."

"And that's of interest because?"

"Guess who was a rookie cop during that time?"

"Him. Right?"

"Right."

"I'm going to presume there's more."

"Smart boy. Although it was more difficult to track, the consensus among the detectives with whom I spoke is that at least six of their unsolveds could just as easily have been categorized as serial."

"And these unsolveds are where?"

"Chicago."

"Ouch."

"There's no proof, though. It's a big-city force suffering a scourge of gun violence. It's not hard to see how an overly taxed department could have missed the signposts. The killings occurred months apart and there were anomalies."

"Such as?"

"Methodology."

"Meaning?"

"They didn't all reflect the same M.O. The one constant was that each of the victims died of a single gunshot wound to the head. Clean. But how and where they met their end was varied. Some were in cars. Others weren't."

"So why would anyone suspect they were serial?"

"Time of day, for one. Place, for another."

"Let me guess. Morning. No spy cameras."

"Bingo."

"So what does that tell you?"

"Nothing concrete, I'm sorry to say. But there's a whole lot of innuendo."

"Did his name come up?"

"You mean as a possible suspect?"

"Yes."

"No."

"No suspicions aroused?"

"None."

"And no one thought to do the drill."

"You mean the comparison drill?"

"Yes."

"Just me."

"So what does that tell you?"

"Nothing to take to the bank, if that's what you mean. Ironically, it's the four killings here that helped point the finger at him."

"How so?"

"Prior to the Freedom killings, there were too many differences and not enough similarities to connect any of the previous investigations. But the trail widens once you look at the Freedom killings."

"Which occurred after the Rockford and Chicago killings."

"Correct. It's only when you place them in the context of those other killings that things start to add up."

"So what now?"

"I'm not certain, Buddy. You're the big-city homicide dick. What do you think?"

"It's complicated. There are any number of things we can do to examine Buzz Farmer's possible connection to the killings. But the most significant ones involve some kind of surveillance. He's very crafty. It will be tough to get anything by him. Particularly anything as noticeable as a surveillance operation.

"As impeccable as these killings have been, they're the product of minute planning and flawless execution. No pun intended. Nabbing him will take nothing short of the same degree of excellence."

"So?"

"So we need to be out in front of him."

"And?"

"Adroit enough to hoist him on his own petard."

FORTY-NINE

Once again I asked Judge Ezekiel Azenberg to provide the warrant.

He sat back in his ancient chair and peered at me over the top of his reading glasses. "You know I've heard from the Governor about this Petrov thing."

"Critically, I presume."

"He was a cipher. The objections are coming from above."

"You mean the Justice Department?"

"Someone's doing everything he or she can to protect Boris Petrov."

"He's guilty, Judge. He's running an opioid lab in his house. Hidden somewhere inside the walls. I've arrested one of his chemists who is prepared to lead me to it. My team is prepped and ready to go. All we need is a warrant."

Judge Azenberg sighed deeply. "You're facing some serious opposition, Buddy. You appear to have rattled a number of compromised cages."

"And your opinion?"

"I'm impressed. You go do what you have to do."

"You mean you'll issue the warrant?"

"It's ready and signed. Pick it up from my clerk on your way out."

"Thank you, Judge."

"Go nail this asshole, Buddy. Show him that not everyone in America is for sale."

• ● ● ● •

We arrived at the mansion at two a.m., barreled our way through the gate, parked in front, and stormed it.

The Sheriff's Department contingent included Al Striar, Dave Balding, Marsha Russo, and Johnny Kennerly. The forensics team came from L.A.

We shot out the lock of the front door, and with Albert Yashin in the lead, we made our way to a small first-floor pantry at the rear of the mansion, adjacent to the kitchen.

We stood facing a floor-to-ceiling wooden glassware cabinet that was painted a dark moss green. It contained all manner of crockery and specialty glasses.

Yashin looked at me, then stepped to the cabinet and pressed his thumb against a small pad, also moss green, practically invisible, on the right side of the cabinet, below one of three metal hinges attached to both the cabinet and to the wall.

Nothing happened.

He looked at me and once again pressed his thumb against the pad, this time more forcefully.

Again nothing happened.

"They've changed it," he said. "This cabinet is controlled electronically, and thumbprint recognition has always been the key to opening it."

"Is the laboratory behind the cabinet?"

"There's a kind of anteroom behind the cabinet. The lab abuts it."

I looked at Johnny Kennerly. "Do it."

Johnny immediately pressed a number on his cell phone and within minutes, one of the forensics techs turned up brandishing a chainsaw.

He looked to me for approval. I nodded.

He proceeded to saw through the cabinet's hinges, causing it to separate from the wall and fall open. He pushed it aside, allowing us access.

Inside was a large anteroom containing a desk, a leather chair, and two wooden filing cabinets. The walls were painted the same dark moss green, as was a door located to the left of the desk. The baseboard moldings and the ceiling were white.

Yashin headed for the door. We followed.

He pressed his thumb against another small pad just below the door's top hinge. This time, the door popped open.

We stepped through it into a large, empty room, painted a glossy white.

Albert Yashin looked at me. "Welcome to the pharmacy. But as you can see, it's been totally stripped."

I turned to Johnny Kennerly. "Put the forensics team to work on it, regardless."

"I'm sorry," Yashin said. "I had no idea they would do this."

Petrov had likely planned this little house-cleaning exercise anticipating we might find it, and had more than likely carried it out in the hours following our disruption of his shipping operation and the seizure of his goods. Which insured that whatever case we were building against him was likely no longer viable.

No evidence. No case.

I was in the throes of feeling sorry for myself when Al Striar sidled up to me. "A word?"

"Sure. What have you got?"

"An anomaly."

"Okay."

"Follow me," he said and walked to a section of the wall on the right side of the room. "Listen to this."

He started tapping on it, producing a hollow sound as if he was knocking on drywall.

"Follow me again."

This time he stepped out of the empty lab and led me to a pair of wooden filing cabinets that stood behind the desk in the anteroom. He pointed me to the right side of the cabinet.

"You see what I see?"

"The filing cabinet is hinged to the wall."

"Tap the wall."

It sounded as hollow as the one in the lab.

"See the green pad located just below the top hinge?"

"I do now."

"What do you make of it?"

"I think we should smash our way through it and find out what's on the other side."

"Excellent call, Buddy. We're so lucky to have as fearless a person as you as our leader."

He grinned and asked Johnny Kennerly to find the chainsaw guy. When he appeared, Striar pointed to the hinges and within seconds, the filing cabinet was separated from the wall.

When we moved it out of the way, we found ourselves staring into a large room filled with the haphazardly stacked equipment and furniture that had clearly been removed from the lab.

We wended our way through a dining room/kitchen and into an office complex replete with a sitting area, a work station with five computer tables, each hosting a top-of-the-line iMac.

Four oversized filing cabinets stood against one of the walls along with a pair of Browning Hells Canyon extra-wide gun safes standing side by side, their steel doors ajar, each safe packed not with guns, but with what appeared to be boxes of opioids.

Three large Picasso lithographs adorned the wall behind a large mahogany desk where in an oversized executive armchair sat none other than Boris Petrov himself.

FIFTY

Petrov surreptitiously sidled over to the twin safes in the hope he might lock their doors.

I thwarted his access, which angered him. He attempted to move around me.

I dodged him.

He glared at me.

I handed him Judge Azenberg's warrant. "You've been served."

"So what? Your warrant is worthless. As are you, I might add."

"You know what, Boris? For a self-described *diplomat,* you display the diplomatic skills of a cretin."

"Let's do without the banter, shall we, Steel? Release me."

"You know, I was preparing to do that. Right up to the worthless comment. Now my feelings are hurt."

"I've had enough of you and your wise mouth, Steel," he said and suddenly stepped up to me and slapped me open-handed in the face.

Although it stung, I held my ground and did nothing.

He attempted to slap me again.

This time I blocked his slap with my left wrist and delivered an open-handed smack of my own. I knew the heel of my hand had dislodged something, even before I saw him spit it out.

Petrov gasped as what appeared to be all of the teeth on the right side of his mouth fell from his head, struck the floor heavily, and fragmented.

"My implants!" he screamed.

He stared horrified at the broken and scattered pieces of teeth. Then he looked up at me. "You smashed my implants," he wailed.

"That's what they were? Implants?"

When he spoke, the right side of his mouth revealed a gaping maw of toothlessness. "Yes, that's what they were, you son of a bitch," he screamed and then rushed me.

Al Striar elbowed his way between us, grabbed a pair of handcuffs from his kit belt and took hold of Petrov's left wrist.

Still livid, Petrov lashed out at him, raking his face with the sharp stone of the ring he wore on his third finger.

Striar's cheek sustained a slashing cut that was now leaking blood, yet he held tight to Petrov's wrist and managed to cuff both of his hands behind him.

Petrov stood screaming at me. "I need to phone my lawyer."

"I'm afraid that's not possible, Boris. You see, you haven't actually been arrested, and you have to have been arrested before you're allowed a phone call."

"I'm injured."

"Not really."

"I require dental attention."

"It would seem so."

We stared at each other in silence.

"Now," he said.

Johnny Kennerly spoke up. "Let me have a look at him."

I shrugged. "I don't know what good it will do."

Johnny stepped over to Petrov. "Smile."

"Fuck you, smile," Petrov shouted, inching away from Johnny.

To me, he said, "You're making another big mistake, Steel. You have no idea how well connected I am. I'll dance on your grave."

"Not unless I'm buried beneath a federal prison."

I called to Al Striar, who was holding a handkerchief to his bleeding cheek. "You need to see a medic. Get things started here and then go. Arrange for all this crap to be impounded. The contents of the lab. Computers. Filing cabinets. And especially the safes. This opioid stash is what's going to bring an inglorious end to Mr. Petrov's illustrious career."

"Will do," Striar said.

"You did good out there, Al. We might have missed this completely if you hadn't discovered the fake wall."

"It sounded flimsy."

"To you it did."

"Anyone could have found it."

"You know something, Al? Accept the compliment and go get your cheek checked."

"I bet you can't say that three times fast."

"Al..."

"Copy that."

FIFTY-ONE

We loaded Boris Petrov into the backseat of my squad car. I climbed in beside him. He was still demanding to see a dentist.

Dave Balding drove us to Victory, a small town in the northern-most tip of San Remo County, where members of the local police force met us and helped settle Mr. Petrov into one of the station's four tiny cells.

When he realized he was being held prisoner, Petrov again started yelling for his lawyer. "You can't hold me like this."

"I can't?"

"I need a dentist."

"A lawyer. A dentist. Is there anything else you need?"

"My implants. What did you do with my implants?"

"They've been entered into evidence."

"Evidence? What evidence? I need them for my dentist."

"I'm afraid that's not possible, Boris."

"You know something, Steel? You have no humanity. You're a deplorable excuse for a human being."

"Deplorable? This from the purveyor of deadly opioids? Deplorable is your middle name, Boris. And you can rest assured your deplorable days here in America are numbered."

He was shouting obscenities at me as I left the area.

• • ● • •

"Skip Wilder on line two," Wilma Hansen said when I responded to her buzz. "He appears to be experiencing an elevated level of 'need to talk immediately.'"

"How do you know?"

"He was yelling."

"Thanks." I picked up the call.

"Another raid?" he asked.

"Successful, too."

"What's that supposed to mean?"

"We accessed the hidden rooms and found the lab equipment, computers with all kinds of Petrov-related business activity on them, plus two giant safes filled with what appear to be boxes of synthetic opioids."

"And that proves what exactly?"

"Too soon to say."

"And if it turns out they prove nothing?"

"Ye of little faith."

"Don't fuck with me, Buddy. Lytell's already had a call from the Governor."

"Was it a nice call?"

"Craig Leonard is hopping up and down. Claims he hasn't heard from his client, despite any number of attempts to reach him."

"And that's of interest because?"

"He says you kidnapped him."

"Who, me?"

"Yes, you. Where is he?"

"I have no idea."

"You best not be lying to me, Buddy. You better not be performing your Jail House Shuffle routine."

"Was there anything else, Skip?"

"Not yet. But I'm sure there will be."

"Then I'll look forward to hearing your dulcet tones again," I said and hung up.

"To what do I deserve this pleasure?" Jordyn Yates asked when she picked up my call.

"I have him."

"And who might *him* be?"

"One guess."

"Boris Petrov?"

"The brass ring is yours."

"Define exactly what *I have him* means."

"I've got him stashed in one of the county jails."

"You're holding him without charges?"

"For the moment, yes."

"Because?"

"We raided his mansion and located several hidden rooms. One of which contained all kinds of laboratory equipment. Another appeared to be Petrov's office which housed a bevy of computers, file cabinets, and a pair of oversized safes filled with synthetic opioids."

"Can you prove it?"

"A forensics team is poring over it all now, and it appears as if we have more than enough to nail him."

"And if you don't?"

"That's what the Assistant District Attorney asked."

"Of course it is. And I'll bet the estimable firm of Leonard, Howard and Arthur is already burning up the phone lines trying to find their client."

"Good bet."

She was quiet for several moments. Then she said, "Judge Lemieux."

"What about her?"

"If you're right, this matter is headed for her courtroom."

"So?"

"I think this might be an excellent time to give her a heads-up."

"Because?"

"Because if you're wrong, you're toast. If you're right, it's going to become a circus."

"So?"

"Before the dam bursts, it might be nice to give the judge a heads-up."

"Which you're prepared to do?"

"The minute I'm off the phone with you."

FIFTY-TWO

"Twice in less than a month," Judge Marielle Lemieux said by way of welcoming Jordyn and me. "Will wonders never cease?"

The judge's chambers were furnished sparingly with painstakingly chosen designer decor. I half expected the brown- and cream-colored sofas and chairs to be covered with protective plastic, but they weren't, and coffee was served boldly by her clerk, despite the risk of spillage.

When we were all properly settled, Jordyn Yates offered, "We're likely facing a shit storm."

"Might I request a bit more specificity?" Judge Lemieux asked.

She was dressed in a black Donna Karan pants suit with an open-necked pink shirt. Her full head of salt and pepper hair was cut short. Apart from a natural lip sheen, she wore no makeup. Her dark brown eyes were agleam with intelligence.

"We expect to be arresting Boris Petrov by the end of the day," Jordyn said.

"Because?"

"A trove of incriminating evidence was found hidden in his mansion."

"Legally?"

"Judge Azenberg's warrant," I said.

"Do you wish to reveal the nature of this evidence?"

"Will the headlines suffice?"

"I'll comment once I've heard them."

"Sources informed us that Petrov was involved in the development and distribution of opioids. Forensics now has proof of it, along with a store of synthetic Fentanyl tablets that were manufactured by Petrov-employed pharmacists, one of whom is in custody.

"We also discovered large sums of cash expertly hidden in the Petrov mansion behind false walls."

"Why are you telling me this?" the judge asked Jordyn.

"I'm guessing Leonard and associates will seek L.A. County jurisdiction. Despite the fact the crimes occurred in San Remo County. But, based on Petrov's notoriety and the influence of his Russian supporters, we're afraid the Governor will agree to this change of venue."

"And?"

"We're going to make every effort to keep it here in San Remo."

"In my court?"

"Yes."

The judge sat quietly for a while. Then she stood. "Thank you, Ms. Yates. I appreciate the heads-up."

Jordyn nodded.

Judge Lemieux turned to me. "I guess what they say about you is true, Buddy."

"And that would be?"

"Trouble goes out of its way to find you."

"You think?"

"I've known you since you were a teen."

"You have."

"So, therefore, I have enough history to opine on such a statement."

"You do."

"I concur."

"About trouble finding me?"

"And vice versa."

"Is that good or bad?"

"Beats me," the judge said with a smile.

FIFTY-THREE

Marsha Russo had asked for an out-of-the-office meeting, so having left Petrov to cool his heels in Victory and awaiting the forensics report, I joined her at Casey's, an upscale burger joint in downtown Freedom.

She had already ordered for us both and was just pouring more vanilla shake from its icy stainless steel container into her now half-empty glass when I dropped down across from her and signaled for coffee.

She stared at me. "Gaunt," she said.

"Sleep deprivation."

"Perhaps you should pay more attention to that condition."

"Have you any other wise nuggets you care to drop?"

"And if I did?"

"I'd have to weigh their efficacy."

"What do you say we can the small talk?" she said taking a large swallow of milkshake.

"You asked for the meeting."

"So I did."

"Hopefully, there's more to it than me having to watch you slurp a milkshake."

She leaned in closer across the table. "I performed a stakeout of the neighborhood in which our most recent victim was found. As you know, it differed somewhat from the kind of location where the three previous killings occurred. It was less upscale, marked not only by commercial properties, but also by residential ones.

"So I made a six-photo composite of potential perps into which I inserted a picture of Buzz Farmer. Then I embarked on a walking tour of the neighborhood and showed the composite to everyone I encountered, both on the street and when I rang doorbells.

"I did it early, at the approximate hour the coroner established as the victim's time of death. In the hope that the morning regulars might have noticed something out of the ordinary. Any kind of anomaly."

"And?"

"I got a hit."

"Meaning?"

"An elderly woman, a dog walker, picked out the photo of Buzz Farmer as someone she'd seen over the course of several days sitting in a parked car across the street from her building."

"Go on."

"She noticed him because he seemed an oddity just sitting there drinking coffee and keeping watch over the goings on."

"Was there anything else?"

"Only that since the murder, he's never reappeared."

"And it didn't occur to her to contact the police and report this strange phenomenon?"

"Actually, it did. But she thought better of it because she had no proof and she believed she'd be dismissed as a crazy old biddy."

"Ageism at its finest."

Our burgers arrived, mine with a side salad, Marsha's oozing melted cheddar cheese coupled with an order of fried onion rings. The waitress served them with a flourish, then hastily disappeared.

Marsha pointed to my salad. "I assumed you were dieting."

I pointed to the onion rings and the whipped cream swirl atop her oversized milkshake. "At least one of us is."

After savoring our initial food foray, Marsha asked, "What do you think?"

"About the burger?"

"About the biddy."

"She was the only person who commented on the photo?"

"Yes."

"Well, it's a start."

"What's that supposed to mean?"

"Let's say the old lady was right and Buzz was lurking around the area. It places him there but it doesn't establish guilt."

"But he was at the scene of the crime before the crime was committed."

"Tough to prosecute."

"But it does raise doubts."

"As do your findings regarding the future ex-Mrs. Farmer."

"So?"

"It's a start, Marsha. A good one. But we need more."

"And how do we go about getting that more?"

"Underhandedly."

"What underhandedly?"

"I've got something in mind."

"You're going to try to get him to incriminate himself?"

"That would be the plan."

"You really believe you can get Mr. Perfection to do himself in?"

"Ain't no such thing as perfection."

"And you're going to prove it?"

"God willing."

"And?"

"And the creek don't rise."

FIFTY-FOUR

"I was wondering when you'd get around to showing up," Sheriff Burton Steel, Sr. commented.

We were on the back porch, he with a gin and tonic, me with water. Although he was still experiencing an uptick in his condition, today he looked tired.

"Are you overdoing it?"

"Why would you say that?"

"Are you?"

"Maybe a little. These meds have had such a positive effect."

The Sheriff sat quietly for several moments, reconsidering the state of his health. Then he admitted, "But it's possible I haven't dealt with their boundaries."

"Meaning?"

"Perhaps I have been overdoing it."

"Then stop."

"Easier said than done."

"Why's that?"

"This business with the Russian. It's got everyone up in arms."

"I'm about to arrest him."

"On what grounds?"

"Forensic evidence."

"Go on."

"We can connect him to the manufacture and distribution of opioids."

"Will it stick?"

"Not my table. I believe we have enough for the DA to make a case. The rest is out of my hands."

"Los Angeles?"

"Not if Judge Lemieux has anything to say about it."

"Does she?"

"Again, it's out of my hands. But she's been given fair warning, and I believe she'll insist."

"And His Eminence Grise?"

"The Governor?"

"Him."

"Hard to tell. It won't be a popular cause for him. Once the case goes public and the press becomes involved, it'll be damned difficult for him to defend Sir Boris. We're talking Fentanyl. Responsible for multiple deaths daily. Governor gets too ardently involved in this case, he runs the risk of self-inflicted political wounding."

"What about the press?"

"Hamstrung."

"Because?"

"Putin, Petrov by association, and the Coastal Commission are anathema. There's no earthly way the press can side favorably with any of them."

We sat silently for a while, listening to the sounds of birds chirping their good nights and crickets awakening.

The Sheriff sighed deeply. "And the rest?"

"You mean the killings?"

"Yes. They're driving Regina crazy."

"A place to which she's no doubt been driven before."

"Don't go there, Buddy."

I flashed the old man my lopsided grin. "I'm wrestling a bear, Dad."

"Buzz Farmer?"

"Yes."

"You think he did it."

"I know he did."

"Why?"

"That's the sixty-four-dollar question."

"What's the sixty-four-dollar answer?"

"He's a psychologically wounded veteran. A victim of post traumatic stress syndrome who somehow managed to deceive himself into believing he's developed a higher calling."

"What calling?"

"Perfectionism."

"Meaning?"

"Somewhere along the line, it became important for him to consider himself the epitome of perfection. He created a private universe for himself. One in which he lived separate and apart from reality. Having learned to kill in Afghanistan, he came to consider killing an art form. And with each subsequent death, he believed he had refined his art to the point of perfection."

"And?"

"He's a sick man, Dad. But I'm close to being able to prove it and put an end to it."

"How?"

"I'm not ready to say yet."

"When will you be ready?"

"On the day I take him down."

"Regina will surely love that day."

"Don't go there, Burton."

FIFTY-FIVE

District Attorney Michael Lytell stormed into Skip Wilder's office, spittle spraying from the corners of his mouth as he bellowed, "Where is he?"

"Who?" I said.

When Wilder stood deferentially, Lytell sat down heavily in Wilder's desk chair. "Already he's being difficult."

Avoiding my amused glance, Wilder reluctantly sat in the chair beside me. "He's here to discuss something with you, Michael. Perhaps you could tone it down a bit and listen."

"Ha," Lytell exclaimed.

"If Boris Petrov is still of interest to you, I might have an answer or two."

"Why is he always so evasive?" Lytell queried Wilder.

"I'm about to arrest him." I answered.

"Petrov?"

"Yes."

"Boris Petrov? You're going to arrest Boris Petrov?"

"And present him to you on a silver platter."

"He's full of shit," Lytell said to Wilder.

"We've got him dead to rights."

"Sure, you do."

"For openers, he's going to be charged with the manufacture and distribution of illegal narcotics."

Lytell stared at Wilder's desktop for several moments, then reached over and rearranged a pile of papers that had been placed scattershot upon it. "And you think it will stick?"

"We discovered incriminating evidence hidden behind fake walls in his home."

"What evidence?"

"I'll present you with the forensic report. And I'll show you the evidence."

"They'll still have him out in no time," Lytell said.

"Not if the judge has anything to say about it."

"What judge?"

"Lemieux."

"What makes you think she would be involved?"

"San Remo County."

"They'll petition for Los Angeles."

"It won't be a slam-dunk for them."

"You think?" Lytell turned to Wilder. "You heard him. It won't be a slam-dunk. I'm so relieved."

Wilder stared at him blank-eyed.

Lytell focused on me. "Why?"

"Why do I think it won't be a slam-dunk?"

"Yes."

"She wants the case."

"Lemieux?"

"Yes."

"You can bet your sweet bippy the Governor will resist."

"He'll be out of it before it even begins."

"What are you talking about?" Lytell said. "Putin's spoken to the Governor personally."

"When he learns the amount of Fentanyl we discovered, he'll disappear faster than Harry Houdini."

Lytell was about to speak again but thought better of it. A silence settled over the room.

"When will this arrest take place?" he asked at last. "It's bound to be a circus."

"It'll happen when it happens."

Lytell looked at Skip Wilder. "Do you understand what he just said? I never understand anything he says."

"Petrov's already in custody." I said. "We'll officially arrest him when the timing is right. No press. No crowds. No lawyers."

"And then what?"

I shrugged. "That'll be up to you."

For a brief moment, Lytell's eyes resembled those of a deer caught in the headlights. Then, just as quickly, he got over it. "What do you propose?"

"Well, for one thing, no bail. As for the publicity, you're the public relations guru. Have a word with Her Honor and make the call."

"This shit is going to hit the fan big-time."

"Rain gear," I said.

"Excuse me?"

"Rain gear will help protect you from the spray."

"He's very funny," Lytell said to Wilder. "Don't you think he's very funny?"

I stood. "My work here is done."

I couldn't get out of there fast enough.

FIFTY-SIX

But I was dead wrong.

The potato was way too hot to handle locally and the Leonard, Howard and Arthur firm, supported by the Governor, pushed the case into the Los Angeles County Superior Court.

The judge, the Honorable James Judith, had been appointed to the bench by the Governor and was quick to seize the opportunity to honor the Governor's wish to have the case play out in the state's highest-profile jurisdiction.

Regrets were tendered to Judge Lemieux, and the L.A. District Attorney's office inherited the proceedings.

I was in the Victory Police Department's headquarters where I happily read Boris Petrov his rights. He glared at me throughout.

"Lawyer," he said, doing his best to conceal his toothless mouth, but not succeeding.

I guided him to the phone and told him he was allowed one call. He picked up the phone and looked at me.

"Privacy," he said.

"No such thing."

"I insist."

"You either place the call now or forfeit your right to make it."

"You, as we say in Russia, are one total shithead."

"Thank you."

He shook his head and dialed. He informed Craig Leonard of his whereabouts and that he had been arrested. Whatever Leonard responded seemed to mollify him. He ended the call and glared at me. "You and I aren't finished, Buddy Steel. You're barking up the wrong bush if you think you can make anything you have on me stick."

"Tree."

"Excuse me?"

"It's tree. Not bush."

Petrov glared at me. "Your time will come Mr. Smart Mouth. Sooner than you think. And when it does, there'll be plenty of rejoicing."

"Will there be party hats?"

I returned his glare with a grin and nodded to Police Chief Art Christensen, who had been watching the proceedings. "Good to go," I said.

Chief Christensen made certain Petrov was properly cuffed and leg-ironed, then led him outside and loaded him into the waiting van. We set off for Freedom where he would be turned over to the State Police.

"You're a loser," Petrov sneered at me.

I didn't say anything.

"You play with fire, you burn to death."

"You're just a fount of malapropisms, aren't you?"

"You chose wrong guy to pick on. You're a dead man walking."

"Come again?"

"You heard me."

"I did. As will the judge, also."

"What's that supposed to mean?"

"You're on tape, bozo. And the judge will be the first person to hear it."

"You recorded me?"

"I did. And not only that, Chief Christensen here heard you, too."

"So what?"

"You threatened the life of an officer of the law. There are penalties for that."

We made the rest of the trip in silence. When we pulled into the courthouse lot, a State Police van was already parked there.

I hustled Petrov into the building and was greeted by a pair of Staties. Captain Alan Hollett presented me with the paperwork required for him to assume responsibility for Mr. Petrov. Marsha Russo assured me that all was in order.

A crusty veteran possessing considerable girth, Hollett set about removing Petrov's bindings. "What happened to his teeth?"

"An unfortunate accident."

"Police brutality," Petrov shouted.

Hollett looked at me questioningly.

I smiled.

Hollett shrugged and glanced briefly at Petrov's mouth. Then he shook my hand, took Petrov by the arm and led him to a waiting vehicle.

After they had gone, Marsha looked at me. "What now?"

"Out of our hands."

"Because?"

"Politics."

"What politics?"

"The Governor insisted this be top shelf, highest priority. Right or wrong, Petrov's arrest will be considered a victory for him personally, elevating his chances for higher office."

"You mean the Presidency?"

"Nothing's higher than that."

"Ironic," she said.

"How so?"

"Collusion with Russians."

FIFTY-SEVEN

The arraignment before the stone-faced Judge James Judith took place early the next morning.

A wan-looking Boris Petrov stood next to his attorney, Craig Leonard, as Leonard petitioned the court to release Petrov to his own recognizance.

The District Attorney's office had sent an Assistant DA to argue on behalf of the State that Petrov should be held without bail.

I was sitting in the empty courtroom alongside Jordyn Yates, having been granted permission to make a statement regarding Petrov's possible release prior to the court's rendering an opinion.

A fair amount of activity was going on at the bench and Judge Judith was glancing at several sheets of paper while at the same time gazing at Petrov and listening to Craig Leonard.

After nearly an hour of this, the judge motioned for the ADA to approach the bench. After several moments of murmured conversation, he looked up and motioned me to the witness stand.

Even though we weren't in the trial phase, the court clerk still swore me in. Once that was done, the judge asked me why I had petitioned the court.

"This was a strange case right from the start, Your Honor," I began.

"How so?"

"At first we were dealing with an abject refusal on Mr. Petrov's part to honor the State law permitting public access to his beachfront property. He had gone so far as to erect permanent, impenetrable barriers, in order to prevent such access.

"He was rebuked by the Coastal Commission and he still refused to allow access. Acting on a request by the Commission, the San Remo Sheriff's Department arranged for the original access points to be re-established. Once that was done, Mr. Petrov's staff re-erected the barriers.

"In the process, it came to our attention that a number of Mr. Petrov's security forces were in the country illegally. Working with Homeland Security, we detained all of these people, most of whom have already been deported.

"At some point, a member of Mr. Petrov's security detail, seeking clemency, informed the Sheriff's Department of Mr. Petrov's involvement with the manufacture and distribution of illegal narcotics. We have photographic evidence of his participation in what turned out to be an aborted attempt to load bagsful of opiates onto several speedboats.

"It was during this action that we became aware of rooms and workspaces in the Petrov mansion that were concealed behind false walls. When we demolished these walls we discovered a hidden laboratory in which a forensics unit determined synthetic Fentanyl had been manufactured. That determination was confirmed by one of the pharmacists involved in the process.

"We also found Mr. Petrov's hidden office which revealed even further incriminating evidence.

"This is the short answer, Your Honor. What greatly alarms the Sheriff's Department is its belief that Mr. Petrov is a threat to flee the country. As a result, the Sheriff's Department recommends that bail be denied him."

"Thank you, Sheriff Steel. The court will surely take your petition into consideration."

I stood and nodded to the judge, but was nearly bowled over by Craig Leonard, who was literally running toward the bench, screaming that I was a liar and a hysteric and that Mr. Petrov is a respected statesman and close associate of Vladimir Putin, blah, blah, blah.

A fair amount of chaos overtook the courtroom and it was then that Jordyn and I made our escape, unnoticed amid the shouting match that was taking place between the legal representatives of both sides.

Once outside, Jordyn looked at me and said, "Gin?"

"In large quantities," I replied.

FIFTY-EIGHT

"It didn't matter," I said to Jordyn.

We were sitting at the bar in the Kwanda Hotel, a short walk from the Stanley Mosk Courthouse on Hill Street. Jordyn was sipping her second martini. I was still on my first.

"What didn't matter?"

"Mr. Judge James Judith couldn't have cared less about anything I had to say."

"Why would you think that?"

"Because his mind was already made up."

"Well, isn't that an indictment of our legal system."

"No. It's a confirmation of the cronyism that exists in our legal system."

"The Governor?"

"Calling the shots."

"Why, do you think?"

"Oh, come on, Jordy. You know better than any of us why."

"But I'd like to think otherwise."

"I'm sure you would, but not in this case."

"Cynic."

"And proud of it."

We finished the dish of peanuts served with our drinks and signaled for another.

"Is it possible this marks the end of my legal services?"

"Unless for some reason Mr. Petrov decides to press charges against me."

"For?"

"God knows. He might argue I was in the wrong when I busted his fake walls and sue me for damages. He might want me to pay for his new implants."

"How likely is that?"

"Not very, given that I'm certain he's going to make bail and then vanish."

"You think he's gonna skip?"

"I know it."

"How do you know it?"

"I'm the Sheriff. I know everything."

"Very funny."

"Of course he's going to skip. You think he's likely to hang around waiting for a trial he's destined to lose?"

"He may not think he's going to lose."

"He's already lost. The proof is irrefutable."

"Says you."

"Meaning?"

"He's connected. He's got powerful lawyers. There's every chance he'll win."

"So maybe I'll wind up having to pay for the implants after all."

We were quiet for a while. The dark of the nearly deserted barroom had insinuated itself into our conversation. The low level background music softened our mood. I looked up to find her staring at me. "I'm at odds with myself, Buddy."

"Which means?"

"You know what it means. It's written all over your face."

I shrugged.

"Oh, come on, Buddy. Here we are. Alone together. In a hotel, no less. Slightly loaded. If for nothing else, we should do it for old times' sake."

"Not going to happen, Jordy. I'd love nothing more than to jump on your bones and I have every confidence it would be as great as it always was. But it didn't work out then and it's not going to work out now."

"Because?"

"We're friends now. And colleagues. I wouldn't want to damage that."

She gazed at me, searching my eyes for any sign of weakness.

"And neither would you, for that matter," I added.

"You know me too well."

"And want to keep it that way."

She finished her martini and I paid the tab. We wandered outside and away from the main entrance of the hotel, where we stood silently for several moments.

She put her arms around my neck.

"I love you, Buddy," she said and kissed me.

"Likewise," I said, intensifying the kiss.

Suddenly we stopped, gazed at each other for several moments, then walked away in opposite directions.

FIFTY-NINE

I was on Highway 101 headed for Freedom when the cell phone interrupted my reverie.

"Buddy Steel."

"He's gone," Marsha Russo said.

"So soon? The judge granted him bail?"

"Who are you talking about?"

"Boris Petrov. He's gone?"

"No. Not Boris Petrov. Buzz Farmer."

"Buzz Farmer is gone?"

Yep."

"How do you know?"

His wife."

"You heard from his wife?"

"She said he phoned and somehow she slipped up and mentioned my visit."

"She told him you had been in Rockford?"

"Yes."

"How did he react to that?"

"She said he took it in stride, whatever that means."

"And now you think he's flown the coop?"

"Not only do I think it, I know it."

"How do you know it?"

"I visited his house. It's empty."

"What empty?"

"Clothes. Personal belongings. Gone."

"Shit."

"Exactly."

"Put out an all-points. Flood the market. Photo. Bio. Everything we know about him. Armed and dangerous, etc."

"I'm on it," she said and ended the call.

"Shit," I said again.

This time to myself.

I had just crossed into Santa Barbara County when the phone rang again. When I picked up the call, Johnny Kennerly said, "He's gone."

"I heard."

"He was on the first plane out of town."

"He was on a plane?"

"Yep."

"How do you know?"

"His gardener saw him come home and then in short order, watched him emerge from the house carrying a suitcase that he loaded along with himself into a limo."

"And he went to the airport?"

"Santa Barbara Municipal."

"And you know that how?"

"The driver told the gardener."

"And he got on a plane?"

"According to the driver."

"Headed where?"

"Initially Nome."

"He was headed for Nome, Alaska?"

"Stop repeating everything I say. Yes."

"Did he arrive in Nome?"

"No."

"What do you mean, no?"

"According to Air Traffic Control, the plane that was originally bound for Nome vanished."

"The plane vanished?"

"According to the flight tower, it did."

"You mean the plane actually vanished from radar detection?"

"Who said that?"

"You said it vanished."

"Of course it didn't actually vanish, Buddy. It veered off of its projected course and headed elsewhere."

"Elsewhere where?"

"The officer at Air Traffic Control said their best guess, since the plane was on a northern trajectory above the Alaska territory, was Siberia. Possibly even Russia."

"You're suggesting Buzz Farmer hijacked an airliner and redirected it to Siberia?"

"Who said anything about Buzz Farmer?"

"You mean this isn't about Buzz Farmer?"

"Of course it's not. We're talking Boris Petrov."

"Boris Petrov left the country?"

"He made bail and fled."

"He made bail?"

"What's the matter with you, Buddy?"

"I hadn't heard anything about the judge even setting bail."

"Two million."

"And Petrov forfeited the two million and bolted?"

"In his private jet."

"Holy crap."

"Leaving behind a shitload of embarrassment."

"Judge Judith set bail at two million dollars?"

"Banged the gavel and left the courtroom."

"And you know this how?"

"It's all over the news."

"Holy crap."

"You already said that."

"Has the Governor chimed in?"

"He expressed his great surprise and regret as to Judge Judith's decision and Boris Petrov's defection."

"And he got away with that statement?"

"So far."

"Is this a great country or what?"

I ended the call and sat stunned in my Wrangler. "Holy crap," I exclaimed yet again.

SIXTY

"Holy crap," my father said when I told him the story.

We were in his office where I had headed as soon as I arrived at the courthouse.

"So now they're both gone," the old man added. "What are the odds of that happening?"

"In hindsight, I'd say pretty good."

Late afternoon sunbeams streaked through the Venetian blinds that were meant to block them out. Dust mites hung heavy in the air, dancing in and out of the light that eked through the slats.

"Meaning?"

"Once the judge decided to grant bail, it was pretty much a certainty that Petrov would bolt."

"And forfeit the two million?"

"Chump change. Once back in Soviet territory, he's safe. At least for as long as Putin's willing to shield him."

"Why Siberia?"

"Easier for him to avoid the spotlight there than in Moscow."

"You think Putin will come after him?"

"Eventually, yes."

"Why?"

"Once it's proven that Petrov was involved in drug trafficking, he's toast."

"But isn't he Putin's guy?"

"He is today."

"And tomorrow?"

"He's safe until Putin is implicated. In time, one way or the other, he will be. It's possible, even likely, he was sharing in Petrov's profits, which were significant. He's known for having his hand in a great many pockets. But he's the President and he'll deny having had anything to do with any kind of narcotics trafficking. His denial will be pronounced and forceful."

"So Petrov will be extradited back to America?"

"He'll be found dead. Allegedly a suicide."

"How do you know that?"

"It's Putin's only play."

"Jesus. And the other guy? Buzz Farmer?" the Sheriff asked.

I stood and began to pace. The dust in the stuffy office had become an irritant and I needed a breath of fresh air. I stepped over to one of the windows, raised the blinds and opened it.

What are you doing?" my father asked.

"Hard to breathe in here."

"You know, I thought that, but didn't do anything about it."

"Well, take a few deep breaths. You'll feel better."

"You haven't answered my question about Farmer."

"He could be anywhere. He prides himself on his perfection. He will have planned for the possibility of escape as meticulously as he did for each of his killings. He won't be easy to find."

I sat back down and wrestled with my thoughts for a while. "As I said before, Buzz Farmer believes himself better than any of us. Smarter. Cleverer. Inviolate. Killing is what he was trained to do, and his psychosis is what guides him."

"This is some farfetched saga."

"It is, isn't it? But whatever the motivation, his preparation and execution were flawless. He struck randomly and without warning. He left zero clues. He learned his trade in Rockport and honed his skills in Chicago. He became more emboldened with each successive killing."

"And then he moved here."

"And, according to his wife, turned totally weird. Distant. Distracted. So much so that she left him. Took their children and slipped out of town while he was on duty."

"Why, do you think?"

"Why was he so weird?"

"Yes."

"He was hiding a huge secret. And fearful of his bubble bursting. He was living an emotional nightmare."

"Fearful of being caught?"

"Frightened he couldn't stop himself."

"But he still managed to fool everyone."

"Maybe. But not his wife. And not Marsha. She put two and two together. She uncovered the fact there were serial killings in each of the cities in which he worked. She sought out his wife."

"And upset his apple cart."

"It was the wife who did that."

"How?"

"By inadvertently mentioning Marsha's visit."

"So that's why he fled."

"And fast, too."

"And you still believe you'll catch him?"

"I do."

"Because?"

"Nobody's perfect."

"Despite his belief that he is?"

"Because of it."

SIXTY-ONE

The call list was prodigious, ranging from legal luminaries to media superstars.

"It's amazing how much in demand you are," Wilma Hansen commented. "A regular Anthony Scaramucci."

"Funny."

"Do you want me to return any of them for you?"

"I'm not going to return any of them."

"Really? Why not? This is your shining moment. You could even make *The View*.

"Not interested."

"Whatever," she said. "See if I care."

I did return the Jordyn Yates call.

"Do you want to hear the list?" she asked.

"What list?"

"The media requests. They appear to have sunk their teeth into the fact you had advised the judge that Petrov was a flight risk, and now they're clambering to get their mitts on you."

"No comment."

"That's your response?"

"It is."

"That's how you want to be quoted?"

"Yes."

"This could be a big moment for you, Buddy. You could go toe-to-toe with the Governor. Create a few ripples in his pond."

"He did what he believed to be the right thing."

"You think the Governor did the right thing?"

"I don't, no."

"Why?"

"Because Petrov is a murderer. Responsible for a great many deaths. But the Governor's a cagey politician. He knew full well Petrov would flee. And, truth be known, I believe he wanted him to flee. Wanted him back on his native soil. The result being no public uproar in California. No overblown trial. No media circus.

"He insisted on Judge Judith because he knew Judith would adhere to his wishes. And he also knew that the minute Judith set bail, Petrov would be gone. He may take some media heat for a while, but in no time the story will be forgotten and the Governor won't have to deal with Petrov singing and dancing his way into America's consciousness. And without having to live through a high-profile trial, he'll still have a clear path to the Presidency. Or at least to the nomination. This was his only option. It's a total win-win for him."

"In what ways?" Jordyn inquired.

"Well, for openers, with Petrov gone, having left behind enough evidence to convict himself, the Governor is free to petition the President to let the State seize the beachfront mansion. Like Obama did with those Russian mansions in Maryland and on Long Island.

"Putin might not be happy about it, but he won't stand in the way. The opioid issue makes it too dicey for him to intervene. So, the government gets the mansion and the Coastal Commission gets to guarantee public access to its beach which, as you may recall, was what drew us all into this mishigas to begin with. On top of which, the Governor emerges smelling like a rose."

"And the media?"

"You mean me and the media?"

"Yes."

"Silence is golden."

"You won't stand up to the Governor?"

"Why would I do that?"

"You'd present a powerful challenge to him."

"Which is exactly what I don't want to do."

"Why not?"

"The usual reason. Commitment issues."

"Oh, come on, Buddy. This could put you in the national spotlight."

"That's all I need. I have no idea what I want to do tomorrow, let alone for the next four years."

She thought for a while before responding. "Okay. I'll ward them all off, if that's what you want."

"Thank you."

"This is very sexy, what you did."

"Sexy?"

"Smart to me is sexy, and for what it's worth, how you've dealt with all of this is very smart. Sexy smart."

"How sexy smart?"

"George Clooney sexy smart."

"Really? George Clooney?"

"Well…let me get back to you on that."

SIXTY-TWO

The media feeding frenzy died down quickly. The story of Petrov's perfidy hit the headlines and occupied the cable news pundits for a few days, then cooled and dropped out of sight. Things in Freedom soon returned to what passed for normal.

In due course, I found the District Attorney's name on my call sheet. ADA Skip Wilder picked up my call. "I bet you were happy to see Petrov's ass flying out of here."

"His and those of the rest of his crowd."

"We're looking into that situation you asked us to."

"Vlad Smirnik?"

"You were right."

"How so?"

"His mother was the child of an American citizen born out of the country. He has a claim on citizenship. We're preparing to argue on his behalf."

"Thanks. He's also going to need some help in relocating."

"Witness Protection?"

"In case the Russians are holding a grudge."

"I'll check it out."

"He cracked the case for us, Skip."

"We understand."

"Was that all?"

"Lytell wants to know more about the serial killings. More about the alleged perpetrator who was on your staff."

"What does he want to know?"

"The full story."

"Okay."

"In Buddy-speak, what does okay mean?"

"He'll have it."

"When?"

"As soon as we can properly prepare it for his consideration. In the meantime, there's a nationwide alert out for him."

"And no further concerns regarding any more possible murders."

"It hasn't been proven that Farmer was the killer. There's evidence that points to that conclusion, but until we can interview him, we have to regard the killings as ongoing and unsolved."

"I'll inform Lytell."

"Thank you."

Wilder was silent.

"May I assume this call is now over?" I asked.

"I suppose."

"Your grudgingly solicitous attitude is duly noted."

"What's that supposed to mean?"

"Figure it out for yourself," I said.

I hung up too quickly to hear his response.

SIXTY-THREE

When I returned to my Wrangler, I found myself sandwiched between a blue Honda Accord that had parked inches from my tail and a red Chevy Cabriolet that was about two feet in front of me.

I was in the downtown jewelry district, having just picked up my father's Rolex from the dealership that had cleaned and serviced it for him.

I began the deking and juking process that would ultimately allow me to maneuver my way out from between the two cars, having dissuaded myself from slapping them both with parking tickets.

I had finally cleared the rear bumper of the Chevy and was just starting to pull into the road when I spotted the black Lexus sedan in my side view mirror, steaming toward me, forcing me to jam on the brakes.

It was only in the seconds before he took the shot that I spotted the barrel of what looked like a Beretta PX4 being leveled at me through the open front passenger-side window by none other than Buzz Farmer.

Reflexively, I ducked below the steering wheel and dropped to the floor, where I found myself face-to-face with the Wrangler's accelerator. I depressed it with the heel of my hand, causing the big SUV to leap forward and clip the rear end of the Lexus as it raced past me, sending it careening into a tailspin.

Farmer's shot went awry, slamming into the back of the Chevy in front of me, as opposed to its intended target, my head.

I righted myself behind the wheel and saw Farmer regain control of the Lexus, race forward and make a left turn at the first intersection.

It took several moments for me to stop shaking and realize he was getting away. Stepping heavily on the gas, I followed him into the turn and found the street in front of me empty.

When I hit the next intersection, I glanced both ways and caught sight of the Lexus in the distance. I turned right and chased it.

I wished I was in my squad car with its light bar and siren, which would have allowed me the chance to move more expeditiously through the mid-morning traffic. I realized I was driving as if in some kind of trance, still trembling, aware of how narrowly I'd missed being shot.

The traffic was heavy. I was in a maze of small streets and multiple intersections. I grabbed my cell and rang the station.

When Wilma answered, I explained what had gone down and that I was in pursuit of Buzz Farmer's Lexus. I asked her to contact all available units, give them my coordinates, and instruct them to locate me and join the fray.

The Lexus was heading toward the freeway. I only realized that it was a different Lexus when Farmer suddenly rammed me from behind, forcing the Wrangler to swerve right and sideswipe several parked cars before screeching to a halt.

As he raced past me, Farmer fired twice, both shots off target. The effort, however, distracted him. The Lexus veered left and clipped the front end of an approaching Toyota Prius, knocking it off course, resulting in it being smacked hard by the Acura sedan behind it.

Farmer jerked the steering wheel and swerved right, narrowly avoiding the two-car accident he had caused. He then accelerated and sped away from the scene.

I was now stopped, confronted by the two drivers whose cars I had sideswiped and scraped. They had leapt from their vehicles and were yelling and pointing at me. With a shrug of regret, I showed them my badge, revved the Wrangler, and sped off after Farmer.

He had transitioned onto Route 32, a four-lane freeway that wended its way west, through the industrial section of Freedom, past multiple factories and warehouses, heading toward interstate Highway One.

Once again I dialed Wilma, this time asking her to arrange helicopter surveillance so we could keep an eye on him from the sky. "I've already lined it up and was just waiting for you to green-light it," she said.

"Light's green."

It wasn't long before I heard chopper noise followed by the appearance of *San Remo Two*, one of the county's four helicopter units.

A pair of squad cars driven by Al Striar and Dave Balding linked up with me as I transitioned onto coastline Highway One, following Farmer as he darted in and out of the fast-moving traffic and heading south.

If he had any hope of escaping the surveillance, he knew by our pursuit and the presence of *Remo Two* above him that evasion had become even trickier. He ratcheted the Lexus up to dangerous speeds.

Although we kept pace, the squad cars and my Wrangler made no effort to overtake him. We were in no danger of losing sight of him. Sooner or later he would either blunder or run out of fuel. Time was on our side.

But as we approached the Pacific beach communities, the traffic grew heavier, forcing Farmer to reduce speed as he maneuvered in and out of lanes.

When I responded to the ringing of my cell phone, Johnny Kennerly asked if Striar, Balding, and I might be able to push Farmer southeast, away from the beach road, toward the Pleasant Avenue turnoff, where Johnny was preparing to string a spike strip diagonally across the road.

"We'll give it a shot."

"I'll get the spike strip in place," he said. "Just be careful that none of you traverse the strip yourselves."

"We're not that stupid."

"Says you."

With *Remo Two* still overhead, the two squad cars and I lined up in a single file on the lane adjacent to the fast one on the left, the one in which Farmer was driving.

After passing him, Al Striar established a position in front of the Lexus, followed closely by Dave Balding, their light bars flashing, sirens wailing. I brought up the rear. As we neared the Pleasant Avenue turnoff, we all began edging further left.

Fearing we might force him off the road, Farmer swerved onto the Pleasant Avenue exit, hurtling forward at speeds approaching a hundred miles an hour.

Striar, Balding, and I slowed, allowing Farmer to put some distance between us, which encouraged him to accelerate even more. He hit the spike strip at an ungodly speed.

All four tires blew out amid a storm of sparks and smoke. Rubber shards flew in every direction. We saw him struggling with the wheel as the Lexus bucked and teetered out of control.

Johnny Kennerly immediately wrested the spike strip from the roadway and we raced on in pursuit of the Lexus, which we saw smash into a guard rail, bounce off and then enter a tailspin that propelled it across the roadway, where it slammed into a pair of parked cars.

Before the Lexus had fully stopped, Buzz Farmer was out of it, the Beretta semi in his hand, racing toward relative safety behind one of the two parked cars.

Striar and Balding skidded to a sideways stop in front of the Lexus, leapt from their respective vehicles and took cover behind them, their service weapons drawn.

I eased the Wrangler to within a few feet of Balding's cruiser, press checked my Colt Commander, and ducked down beside him.

We were on a cliffside overlooking the Pacific, in a neighborhood that boasted some of San Remo County's costliest homes. The commotion had attracted a handful of curious residents, one of them photographing the events with her cell phone. Striar hollered for them to take shelter.

Several cars were parked in front of a gated mansion and it was there, from behind a Subaru Outback, that Farmer got off an opening salvo of six shots, two of which slammed into Balding's squad car.

In a moment of quiet, I called to him. "Buzz. It's Buddy. Throw down your weapon."

"Fuck you, Buddy."

"Don't risk being shot, Buzz. Put it down."

"You ruined everything," he hollered, his voice scratchy and weary.

"We can talk about it. I can get you help. Put down the gun and come out."

"How did you find out?" he shouted. "How did you know?"

"The three cities."

"What difference would they have made?"

"Enough to provide a link."

"That's a crock, Buddy. It had to be something else. The methodology in each of those cities was different enough to prevent any such link."

"Surrender peacefully and I'll tell you."

"It was something I did, wasn't it?"

"Give it up, Buzz."

"There isn't a snowball's chance in hell those killings could have been connected."

"I'm not going to argue with you."

"It was something else. Or someone else. What was it?"

I remained silent.

"Come on, Buddy. What was it? Was it my wife? Was it Kelly?"

"Surrender, Buzz. Don't let this turn sour."

Farmer didn't speak for a while. He peeked around the corner of the Lexus, assessing his chances of escape. Then he stepped out, holding his Beretta by his side.

"I'm not going to jail, Buddy."

"Put the gun down, Buzz. We're all of us here your friends and are greatly saddened by this. We'll treat you with the respect you earned during your service with us. We'll make certain you get the best psychiatric care."

"Don't bullshit me, Buddy. I'm a fucking serial killer, for God's sake. Treat me with respect? I don't think so."

"You're wrong, Buzz. You have my word."

He glared at me, raised the pistol and placed it against his forehead.

SIXTY-FOUR

Once again I was in the news and once again I declined requests for interviews and appearances. I credited Marsha Russo with having identified Buzz Farmer as the serial killer and the media swarmed her.

"How did it turn out that I've become your media representative?" Jordyn Yates said when I picked up her call. "Prior to my agreeing to represent you, I was a highly regarded attorney in a very prestigious firm. Now, instead of client calls, I'm fielding requests from the likes of Anderson Cooper and Sean Hannity."

"Congratulations," I said.

"Don't smart mouth with me, Buddy. You have no idea how time-consuming it is for me and my staff."

"Bill me," I said.

"That's not the point."

"So what exactly is the point? Other than the opportunity for me to listen to you whine."

"You're a fucking hero, Buddy. Everyone wants a piece of you."

"Not interested."

"You're nuts. You're a national phenomenon. Sheriff Buddy Steel. Brings down a Russian drug cartel and a serial killer both in the same week."

"Coincidence. On their own, neither is newsworthy."

"Will you at least grant one interview? Stephanopoulos? Norah O'Donnell?"

"I might consider James Corden. But only if I can sing in the car."

"Is there any chance you might take this a little more seriously, Buddy?"

"It's already a done deal. But I will hire a publicist to fend them all off."

"No, you don't have to do that. I'll still rep you."

"I never meant to be a burden, Jordy."

"I know," she said. "But it was worth the try."

After a brief silence, I offered, "May I tell you something? Something in confidence."

"I'm your lawyer, aren't I?"

"I'm thinking of dropping out for a while."

"Meaning?"

"I want off the grid."

"Stop being obtuse, Buddy. What are you talking about?"

"I've had my fill of this circus. I need to stop the world for a while. Take some time for myself."

"Because?"

"I feel rudderless. Untethered to any recognizable reality."

"And you think time out will change that?"

"It might."

"And where are you thinking of taking this time out?"

"I don't know."

"What is it you want to do?"

"That's just it. There's nothing I want to do. Go for a hike, maybe. Climb a mountain."

"Utah."

"Excuse me?"

"I own a ski cabin in Utah. In Deer Valley. I'm not using it. You can have it."

"You mean I can stay there?"

"Yes."

"Can I get back to you on that?"

"Whenever."

"Thank you."

"You're sure about this?"

"Yes."

"You're really willing to step away from the spotlight?"

"I am."

"Forgive me for being so old-fashioned. Missed opportunities never fail to haunt me."

"*Leave the gun. Take the cannoli.*"

"Excuse me?"

"*Leave the gun. Take the cannoli.*"

"What are you talking about?"

She was quiet for several moments, then she said, "Wait a minute. I get it. I know this game. I love this game. *The Godfather*, right?

I knew she was grinning without seeing her.

"It's a line from *The Godfather*. I know it is. I know more lines, too. How about, '*Luca Brasi sleeps with the fishes?*'"

When I said nothing, she went on. "*He was banging cocktail waitresses two at a time.*"

"Jordyn…"

"*They shot Sonny on the causeway.*"

"Jordyn…"

"I'll take lines from movies for forty, Alex."

SIXTY-FIVE

The specter of Buzz Farmer's death haunted me. When I closed my eyes, the vision of him shooting himself blotted out everything else.

I blamed myself for not having been more forceful. For not being skillful enough to have prevented what occurred. My nights were filled with remorse, my days with distraction.

My rational self argued there was no way I could have thwarted Farmer's suicide. I wasn't the threat that caused him to kill himself. He had turned out not to be the image of perfection he had fashioned for himself. And that, he couldn't live with.

My irrational self charged me with failure. Petrov escaped prosecution. And, in retrospect, Farmer did, too.

Despite the media veneration, I saw myself as having botched the job. And, instead of facing media adulation, what I was really facing was my steadfastly unforgiving conscience.

And, just as my father was experiencing a respite from the inevitability of his fate, I was staring eye-to-eye at mine.

● ● ● ● ●

I stepped off the plane in Chicago, rented a Chevy Camaro, and drove to Rockport. I parked in front of her house and sat there for a while.

It was one of a community of modest homes, all crowded together in a lower-middle class neighborhood, on narrow streets that often doubled as playgrounds and makeshift clubhouses.

Finally I navigated the short cement walkway and the three steps that led to the front door. I rang the bell.

When she opened it, I realized I had seen her before. At the Ralph's market in Freedom, examining canned goods further down the aisle from where I had unexpectedly run into her husband. He had never thought to introduce us and I hadn't put two and two together until this moment.

"Sheriff Steel." She offered her hand. "Kelly Farmer."

"Mrs. Farmer."

"Will you come in?"

"Thank you." I followed her inside.

She was kind-looking, at ease within herself, and pretty in an understated way. She wore no makeup. Hers was a narrow face, full lipped with a slightly upturned nose and a ruddy complexion that emphasized the intensity of her moist brown eyes.

She showed me into a small living room that was also a repository for a great many children's toys and accessories, as well as a tiny playpen, currently unoccupied.

"Nap time," Kelly Farmer explained. "We'll need to keep our voices down."

I nodded. We sat.

"Why?" she asked.

"Why am I here?"

She nodded.

"To pay my respects."

"You didn't need to do that."

"I know. But there was something unfinished between me and Buzz. Something unspoken that didn't exactly end with his death."

"Such as?"

"I haven't actually articulated it before. I hope I can make myself clear."

Again she nodded.

"I was one of those who was in favor of his coming to Freedom. Perhaps it was the bill of goods he sold me regarding how much he wanted his family out of Chicago and away from a big city. I keep wondering what it was about him that got to me."

"He had a way of doing that, of getting to people. Ever since he was a kid."

"Well, he surely got to me. In hindsight, I think it was because he seemed so devoted to his work. He took things seriously and spared no effort in his quest to be perfect at each and every turn."

"You noticed," Kelly said. "That was his parlor trick. He always made people believe his faux seriousness."

"You think it was a trick?"

"I do. I think it was a more complicated trick than what met the eye. It wasn't about his seriousness regarding the job, his quest to be perfect, as you put it. It was his seriousness as it applied to him succeeding at his con. Making you believe he was the best there was, when all the time it was about pulling the wool over everyone's eyes regarding what he was really up to."

"Killing people."

"Not just that. It was how he killed them. The level of preparation and expertise it took. And making sure no one ever caught on. My shrink refers to it as his psychosis."

"Your shrink?"

"My psychiatrist. Thanks to my parents, I've been seeing her ever since I got back here."

She withdrew into herself for several moments.

I watched her consider what she wanted to say next, discard the first thoughts that crossed her mind, then settle on it. "He fooled me. For the longest time. I'm in analysis to learn how that could have happened. And to prevent it from ever happening again."

"And the children?"

"The baby's too young to know anything other than he's no

longer here. Burton Junior is four, though, and he keeps asking when his daddy will be coming home."

"Burton, Junior?"

"Yes. After his father."

"Buzz's name was Burton?"

"It was."

"Mine too."

"Your name is Burton?"

"Burton, Junior."

"But they call you Buddy."

"Yes."

"Buddy and Buzz. Nicknames. What an odd coincidence."

"Yes."

"What is it that brought you here?"

"He haunts me."

"He fooled you, too."

"He was very good at it."

"He was."

After an awkward silence, I asked, "How are you faring?"

"With my shrink?"

"With your life."

"I know there's light at the end of the tunnel. I just haven't spotted it yet."

"But you will."

"Yes. And I also believe I'll be a better person and mother once I do."

"He told me his death would be on my conscience."

"Of course he did."

"It was the last thing he ever said."

She chuckled. "And you bought it?"

"I might have."

"Get over it, Buddy. May I call you Buddy?"

"Better than Burton."

"Don't stay caught up in his game. He knew there was no

other way out. He would have been bonkers had he gone to jail. This was his exit strategy. As carefully planned as was everything else in his life. Don't buy it, Buddy. He set you up in the hope you would. That you'd suffer because of it."

I considered all she was saying and somewhere inside, I knew it was true. He set me up to be his victim.

"Thank you, Kelly. You're right, of course."

"Funny," she said.

"What is?"

"Gullibility. We believe what we want to believe and everything else be damned."

"Even when we know it to be wrong."

"Especially then."

SIXTY-SIX

I slung my duffel into the backseat and slipped into Johnny's car.

He was parked in front of a gate at the rear of the property that offered access to the gardener's shack. The real estate manager had provided me with a key, in large part because the gate was not within eyesight of the building's main entrances and thusly afforded unnoticeable egress.

I ducked down as Johnny stepped on the gas and swept us away from the building before any of the media throngs could react.

"What's with the duffel?" Johnny asked.

"I'll tell you when we get there."

"Get where?"

"The courthouse."

"That's where I'm taking you?"

"And hopefully a whole lot faster, too."

We slipped into the underground parking garage and headed for my office, where Marsha Russo joined us.

"I'm taking a sabbatical," I announced.

"You're what?" Marsha exclaimed.

"I'm going to disappear for a while."

"Disappear where?"

"Wherever the four winds blow."

"Does he know?" Johnny asked.

"He will in about twenty minutes."

"He won't be happy."

"He'll get over it."

"I'm serious, Buddy. Why are you doing this?"

"Between us, my head hurts. It was one thing when the old man's trajectory was a straight line to his destiny. Now that it's uncertain, which, by the way, pleases me no end, I see an opening for a little offline reflection.

"He won't understand, but in truth, this ride I'm on has no boundaries. No time constraints. No respite. So, before I go completely bonkers, I'm going to seize the moment and get off it for a spell.

"In the words of Ayn Rand, I plan to examine my premises and pray I find answers that will enhance my prerogatives."

Johnny and Marsha exchanged glances.

"For how long?" she asked.

"Not long."

"And you're dropping this hotcake onto my lap," Johnny said.

"Life's a bitch, ain't it?"

I found him in his office, seemingly robust, the beneficiary of the experimental drug regimen. "My son the headliner," he joshed.

"The reluctant headliner."

"You've become a local legend, Buddy. It's time to accept it and allow fate to embrace you."

"No."

"What no? You're on a trajectory straight to Sacramento."

"No."

"I'm serious, Buddy. There's talk of you succeeding the Governor."

"I have no interest in becoming Governor. Or of holding any

elected office, for that matter. I came here to assist you, and now that you're doing so well, I'm heading off for a little R and R, rest and reconsideration."

"What are you talking about?"

"I have to get away from this circus, Dad. From the politics and the unwanted attention. I watched a corrupt Russian opioid purveyor, whom I jumped through hoops to apprehend, make bail for some cockamamie political reasons and then predictably flee the country.

"I saw a Sheriff's Department deputy blow his brains out as a means of achieving revenge against me for uncovering the fact he was a psychotic serial killer.

"Frankly, it's worn me out. So, I'm done for a while. When I agreed to come here I had no idea what I was in for."

"You can't be serious, Buddy."

"I'm serious."

"But surely you'll come back once this episode of yours calms down."

"It's likely."

"But not certain."

"Fairly certain."

"But not wholly."

When I said nothing, he went on. "What will I do without you?"

I knew it was only a matter of time before it became about him.

"Johnny's here," I said by way of mollification. "And, in the long run, he's far better suited for the job than I."

"That's a load of crap and you know it."

"Maybe. But that's how I see it."

"What if I insisted you stay?"

"Wouldn't make any difference."

The old man remained silent.

"I love you, Dad. More now than ever. You're in the best

shape you've been in for a while. Everyone here adores you and you have an excellent staff. Run your show. Because that's what it is. Your show."

"How will I find you?"

"Cell phone."

"And you'll answer it?"

"I promise."

I stood as did he. We embraced. There were tears in both of our eyes. I gripped his hand and kissed his cheek.

Then I hurriedly left the office and raced down to the car park where Johnny was waiting.

He revved the engine as I climbed in. "How did it go?"

"He knows."

"And he's okay with it?"

"Let's just say he knows."

The gloom of the garage gave way to bright sunshine as we sped away from the courthouse. "Where to?" Johnny asked.

"Freedom."

"The airport or the state of mind?"

"Both."

SIXTY-SEVEN

The key was where she said it would be. The cabin was located steps from a ski run, on a mountainside bordered by a vast forest, beneath a crystal clear sky.

It had been constructed of rough-hewn logs and mortar. Small yet accommodating. Thick, colorful Indian rugs blanketed the redwood plank floor in an open space that contained a sitting corner, a dining area, and a kitchen.

A pair of well-worn sofas, two overstuffed armchairs, and three mismatched tables fronted a brick-lined walk-in fireplace. The dining area hosted an oval oak table with six ladder-backed armchairs. It abutted a pale blue-and-white-tiled kitchen that featured an ancient O'Keefe & Merritt four-burner stove and a relatively new Maytag fridge.

The bedroom boasted a queen-sized bed, a pair of wooden night tables, a dresser, and an ample closet. A whirlpool bathtub and shower combo monopolized the better part of the small bathroom. A sink, a toilet, and a bidet rounded out the balance.

I threw my duffel onto the bed and stepped out the back door through a tiny changing hut and onto the ski run. The windblown aroma of the surrounding forest invaded my senses.

This was Jordyn's sanctuary. Where she sought refuge. Where she rediscovered herself and found the energy to plow forward.

I felt at home here and understood that what Jordyn found in her mountain retreat was what I had been seeking, too.

● ● ● ● ●

After a visit to Park City, where I loaded up on food and drink, I strapped on my hiking boots and headed off into the hills.

A hint of winter was in the air and a few snow flurries swept over me. I experienced a sense of relief. As if a huge weight had been lifted.

I hiked the hills for three-plus hours. Despite the chill, I broke a sweat. I looked forward to a hot bath. By the time I reached the cabin, the sun had already begun its descent.

I filled the tub, shed my clothes, and settled my aching bones into the steamy whirlpool where I spent nearly an hour.

I was drying off and thinking about dinner when I thought I heard the cabin door open.

I hastily tied the towel around my waist and stepped into the bedroom where I discovered Jordyn Yates lifting her suitcase onto the bed.

"Surprise," she said.

I stared at her slack-jawed. Then the towel fell off.

"Your fly is open," she snickered.

I clumsily picked up the towel and did my best to cover myself. "What are you doing here?"

She tossed a copy of *The Los Angeles Times* onto the bed. Its headline read, *RUSSIAN BILLIONAIRE FOUND DEAD IN SIBERIA*.

"You sure got that right," she gloated.

"Yeah, well, kudos for me. Why are you here?"

"I wanted you to see the paper."

"That's why you're here?"

"Yes."

"No, it's not."

"Yes, it is."

"Tell me why you're really here."

"I needed a rest."

"You needed a rest?"

"Yes."

"Did you forget you had lent the cabin to me?"

"Not at all."

"You mean you came here on purpose."

"I did."

"Knowing I was here."

"Yes."

"Why?"

"Because I disagree with your assessment."

"What assessment?"

"The assessment of our relationship…past and present."

"In what way?"

"In every way."

"So, that being the case, what happens now?"

"You use your imagination is what happens now," she said as she wrested the towel from my grasp and wrapped her arms around me.

Acknowledgments

WITH GRATITUDE...

...to the amazing Poisoned Pen Press team...Diane DiBiase, Holli Roach, and Beth Deveny,

...to the indefatigable Michael Barson,

...to the indispensable Annette Rogers,

...to the incredible Barbara Peters,

...and to Robert Rosenwald, who continues to make the trains run on time.

And, thanks to Steven Brandman, Miles Brandman, Roy Gnan, and Melanie Mintz,

...to my longtime friend and partner, Tom Selleck,

...with special thanks and love to Tom Distler,

...and to Jeffrey, Selma and Arthur Brandman, who inspired and nurtured the dream.